ANANCY'S SCORE

BOOKS BY ANDREW SALKEY

Anancy, Traveller
Caribbean Folk Tales and Legends edited and compiled by Andrew
Salkey
Anancy's Score by Andrew Salkey

Other titles published by Bogle-L'Ouverture Publications Ltd
Danny Jones
The River that Disappeared
Joey Tyson
Writing in Cuba since the Revolution
The One: The Story of how the people of Guyana avenge the murder
of their Pasero with help from Brother Anancy and Sister Buxton
Jamaica: An epic poem exploring the historical foundations of
Jamaican society

Anancy's Score

by

ANDREW SALKEY

BLP

Published by
BOGLE L'OUVERTURE PRESS
64 Gifford Street, London N1 0DF

Published by BOGLE-L'OUVERTURE PRESS (1992)
First published by Bogle-L'Ouverture Publications Ltd

ISBN 095015 468 7

BOGLE L'OUVERTURE PRESS
64 Gifford Street, London N1 0DF

Printed in Great Britain by
Redwood Press Limited, Melksham, Wiltshire

To
Jessica Huntley
and
Accabre Huntley

ACKNOWLEDGEMENTS

Acknowledgements are due to the following in which some of the stories in *Anancy's Score* have previously appeared : *Poetry Quarterly*, edited by Wrey Gardiner; *Deutsche Zeitung*, a German daily newspaper; *Westindien*, a German anthology of West Indian short stories, edited by Janheinz Jahn; *Black Orpheus*, a Nigerian literary magazine, edited by Ulli Beier; *Black Orpheus*, an anthology of African and Afro-American prose, edited by Ulli Beier; *Political Spider*, an anthology of African and Caribbean short stories, edited by Ulli Beier; *Miscellany Six*, an annual anthology of prose and poetry, edited by Edward Blishen; and *Commonwealth Short Stories*, an anthology, edited by Anna Rutherford and Donald Hannah.

Acknowledgements are also due to the following on whose literary programmes some of the stories have been broadcast : the Nigerian Broadcasting Corporation and the British Broadcasting Corporation.

AUTHOR'S NOTE

Where would Afro-Caribbean folk tales be without the seminal support of the African Anancy? Indeed, how could this book ever have been written without it, or without Anancy's historical authority, or without my having tapped Anancy's score in his first home country?

The traditional Anancy is a crisp, cool, calculating spider, a persuasive, inventive, anarchic spider-man.

I have wilfully used his name, and even more wilfully tried to understand his nature, and remoulded it for my own ends.

I have plucked my Anancy from the great folk tales of West Africa and the Caribbean, and I have made him inhabit both worlds, the old and the new, locked deep in my own imagination; he also inhabits the ready minds of children, and crashes the defences of most adults. He holds no reservations; makes only certain crucial allowances; he knows no boundaries; respects no one, not even himself, at times; and he makes a mockery of everybody's assumptions and value judgements.

In this personal collection, the language and the plots are mine; and the twists, turns and flights of invention are also mine. The journey and the critical eye are yours.

A.S.

CONTENTS

How Anancy became a Spider Individual Person ... 13
Political Spider 31
Anancy and the Ghost Wrestlers 43
Anancy, the Sweet Love-powder Merchant 53
Vietnam Anancy and the Black Tulip 61
Anancy, the Spider Preacher 69
Anancy and the Queen Head 81
Anancy, the Atomic Horse 89
The Man Name Peacefulness 95
Peace Meal Anancy 101
Seventeen 107
Gold, Silver and Brass 113
Soot, the Land of Billboards 117
In Yessing Mount 123
Spider Hell Hole 129
Anancy, People Painter 135
Anancy, Don't Give Up! 143
Anancy not no Pyaa-Pyaa Spider Man come from Bal-
carres F'get a Gardener Job from a Brown 'Oman
Livin' in a Big Ol'-time Boa'd 'Ouse up a Sain' Andrew
Top 157
A Real, Real Short Story as to How Anancy Actual Reach
Up Through F'him One Wife to Equal Life with
all Total 'Omankind, Baps! 167
New Man Anancy 173

It was in language that the slave was perhaps most successfully imprisoned by his master; and it was in his (mis-)use of it that he perhaps most effectively rebelled. Within the folk tradition, language was (and is) a creative act in itself; the word was held to contain a secret power . . .

Edward Brathwaite   From *Folk Culture of the Slaves in Jamaica*

HOW ANANCY BECAME A SPIDER INDIVIDUAL PERSON

HOW ANANCY BECAME A SPIDER INDIVIDUAL PERSON

Once, when neither mushrooms on the ground nor mushrooms up in the air were killing off people, when trees were honestly trees, when things used to happen as if they hadn't any good reason not to happen, when time was just time, there were plenty chances for small animals to grow into big animals without being maimed along the way. There were plenty chances for animals to have lots of green space to romp about and jump up and down all over the place, like dove feathers, without direction or caution. As a matter of fact, all the animals and trees and everything had a magical, straightback dignity of bearing, as if they were special, free creatures and things on the lan'. All this used to happen in a place called The Beginning.

The Beginning was a peculiar, nice feeling of a place for total most living things. Why 'most', and not 'all' total living things? Well, it was like that really : one or two inhabitants of The Beginning had problems, even though problems weren't problems as we know them nowadays.

The Beginning was the mystery beginning of all the present muchness, all the inside feelings and outside actions. The Beginning never had the slightest cause to pin down the inhabitants to narrow code of this or narrow code of that. It had only one serious word to say about a certain tree. That tree was big, everlasting and spreading, as if it had a whistling, silent importance resting hidden inside its trunk and leaves and branches. If you looked up and saw that tree, you would begin to imagine it might talk to you. But that was the shyness of the nature of the tree; it never talked, at all; it never talked because it had too much to say. It knew heaps. It stood tall and quiet, and swayed a little, but that was all; it never spewed out any of its high knowings, as if they were common, street knowings.

It happened now that one daytime when Brother Sun was stretching far up into the big blue, Brother Anancy and his wife

13

were walking up and down the banana field in the place called The Beginning. You might think that the name of this total garden is a funny coincidence of a name, but that is the personal business of all names. Names must lead people on and cause a lot of botheration. Believe me : there's no other way that names and tags can serve any purpose, particularly when people looking up to names and tags, and using them to settle affairs for all time. People trap names and treat them as final judges. Now, Brother Anancy was the sort of hunter who behaved like a silent partner attached to yet another silent partner who had never once turned up at board-meeting no time at all. And Brother Anancy wife? Well, she was a cute, sharp creature, whistle thin and fast-eye bad. She was born with a fat appetite to taste experience, as if she was a Boss 'Oman in charge of a whole heap of plantation workers, chiefly washerwomen and during the week cooks.

Listen to the lip she's lashing Brother Anancy with cold : " I talkin', now, Anancy. You too much of a spineless dead 'ead crowbait. You couldn't even run a race with a snail an' beat it."

Anancy is a swallow hard 'usban', a knock softly. Not an answer is an answer. His wife can talk a stream and know that things will always be the same with Anancy. Life must go on. A wife is a life.

" There's no use my hopin' you goin' be the builder of the house of my children. All you want to do is stay right here in The Beginning an' live rent free an' drink water-coconut an' eat bake bananas. Pure freeness you in love with; not me. Even though you walk roun' the place with a stiff backbone, as if you the original proud t'ing, you got no spine as far as I concern, an' I concern plenty. You a tall, long foot naked somet'ing crawlin' over the lan' with a hungry belly an' two green starin' eyes hangin' out of a thick nonsense 'ead. You an' you slow ways make me sick for true. All this dignity-t'inkin' jus' makin' me wish I didn' know you never."

Brother Anancy trying to say something, now. Mouth-screwing going on and body-scratching following fast, as if he's infested with tickling insect thoughts. But nothing don' go so. Anancy is a scratcher because of white nerves, as though somebody superior asking to talk to him, and poor Anancy unable to

14

face the superior person, as though big 'fraid holding him back from doing that little thing. Somehow, Brother Anancy always ending up trembling when his wife in a talking mood, and trembling when she not. The two of them enjoying all through the years a sort of employer-employee coin, if you spin and catch the meaning. So, that being that, Brother Anancy deciding to take a chance on life. He says, " You know somet'ing, 'oman? "

" I don', 'usban'-man. You tell me."

" You a mos' impatient 'oman on the lan'. That's what I know."

" That's all you got to tell me, Anancy? "

" That's too much already."

" So *you* say."

" You see how everyt'ing spreadin' out roun' us? Lots of secret organization had was to go into it, you know."

" So? "

" So there's a time to settle down like sediment an' a time to make movement like John Crow. My time to move don' come yet. Don' rush t'ings like the busy 'oman you born to be."

" You goin' dead from talk one of these days, Anancy. You know that? "

" Don' bother youself how I goin' dead. You come an' see t'ings organize in front of you, an' you got to leave them so. Wait an' witness the harvest of t'ings. For all you know, plenty t'ings in store for us to make a house an' settle down independent like. But because haste an' quick move catchin' you eye, you will spoil the benefits comin' down to us."

Brother Anancy wife jumps in smart-up and full of fire-eyes. Hear her, now : " Why you always sayin' that word, Anancy? "

" Which word? "

" You know. ' Benefits comin' down '."

" Oh, that ! "

" I goin' tell you a t'ing. Not a blasted t'ing ever come down but rain. Only rain water comin' down from Up. Up is a place that don' even begin to exis' yet. You forecastin' or what? "

"I t'ink you frighten."

" Only you dreamin' 'ead believe so, Anancy. You seein' signs before they come. One time, you talk about good and evil;

15

then another time, you talk about fallin' from grace; then you madness tell you that one day we goin' have to cover up our naked self an' run like black ants an' leave the banana field an' leave The Beginning forever."

" That's right."

" So, nuh? Firs' of all, what is the meanin' of nakedness? How you know that we possess such a t'ing? Who tell you? "

" You don' trouble how I know an' who tell me. We neat an' naked, an' that is that."

" Neat an' naked, nuh? "

" Sure, 'oman."

" Well, Anancy, I want you to hold careful some facts in that basin head you got on you bare back. You wearin' me out with you forever worry head. You makin' me feel half o' 'oman with you watchin' an' peepin' an' t'inkin' roun' corners about this an' that. You makin' me wonder if you not a mad, moonshine 'usban'. The one piece o' rib from you side that help to born me in this place come from you mad set o' ribs, an' I sure it catchin' like plague. But like how I can't give it back to you, I suppose I got to live with it for better or worser."

" You a mos' ungrateful woman."

" You a 'usban' I could well do without."

" Do without me then nuh."

" An' imagine : I have to know you in me naked state."

" So, you usin' me word, then? "

" You tell me so many times that I bound to know about nakedness, even if it live only in me mind."

After her woman back chat, Brother Anancy tryin' to make a come back with a big speech to settle her hash for one time definite. This is a painful thing for Anancy to do, but he is a chance taker on certain matters. In the long try, he beating all his doubts and hesitating and backing-back, and he getting plenty courage. Hear the big flow : " You hard to live with, 'oman. We got space to lose each other like not'ing, an' I can't lose you out of me mind at all. Why you don' hold on to you appetite for t'ings I can't provide for you? I suppose one of these days you goin' want me to do the impossible action, like climbin' the serious tree an' eatin' the luscious red fruit growin' on it? "

16

His wife starting to move in on him with a cool vengeance. Her eyes blazing tactics. Her nose quivering a whole branch of leaves. Her mouth looking wicked. This is the bite now : " How many times I got to tell you that t'ings like trouble don' invent yet? You seem to have a sort of firs' look at t'ings that don' create. You always talkin' in a way that not even in swing. You causin' me to sick up to me neck with you. Live on the lan' easy, nuh. You goin' on as if you the conscience of the whole total place. If you settin' up youself as a conscience man, then, let me tell you right now : ' don' want to lie down an' have to nice-up to no conscience when night-time come roun'. If conscience you want to give me when body call, then, I goin' start lookin' for a body to answer body call."

Anancy is an expert shock-absorber. He knows his wife is a brass-face talker and a storehouse of ace hole bad talk. Looking around The Beginning and smiling a funny absorber smile, he hears himself saying : " I don' understan' that sort of new t'inkin' at all, 'oman. So what's all this business about nice-up when night-time come roun'? "

" Never mind, you garden fool, you. That is just my way of doin' a bit of forecastin' where night-time an' we concern. Look at it that way, nuh."

She's trying to say something else, but Brother Anancy slipping off into one of his sweet day-time dreams, walking light and floating with his head strolling in total dignity, as if one thing is the earth and the other is the free air, with no fall in it no how.

Anancy wife is walking in the opposite direction and making some deep footprints. There she is puffing and blowing a heap of vexation and 'oman-temper, as different from man-temper, as the world should well know by this time. Her head is an echo-box of shaking shapes and sounds, with scorn and mockery turning over and over like dice. When she's listening to the echoes, a feeling of dark eye and tiredness starting to circle her life in The Beginning. She's walking nearish to the serious tree. She's hearing a noise up in the branches. She's looking up, now, and her neck-string is standing right up to bursting point, with her neck-column showing a maze of small muscles and veins. The noise is a long snake is a kind of voice saying something sing-song. And this is it : " If you're not satisfied with your lot, just come and talk things over with me. Talk to me. Talk to me. Talk to me."

Now, we must leave Anancy wife alone, because it's not a good thing to listen to a private conversation, especially when it is a first chat between a married 'oman and a snake up in a tree. We might hear the sort of labrish to make us wish we didn' cock ears at all. Don' you know how it is? Secret servicing is a bitch.

We're going after Anancy, now. He's far away by this time. His walking taking him far down to the bottom of The Beginning. He's standing up like a poet-being in the open, looking tender and sympathetic at the running waters of the streams and the flowers and the insects, shifting, trembling and living round him. I say the word ' poet ' because, even though that odd kind of person hasn't been created yet, Anancy, in all his worries, is actually getting on like one, looking that way and promising to burst open with a white light shooting rays all over the place. By the way, it's a good thing to remember, from now onwards, that a poet, when the time and the garden space come to make that oddment of person, will really be nothing more than a half-happyman and half-worrier, the kind of person who will be celebrating and fretting, all at the same time, about things like the running waters of the streams and the flowers and the insects and creatures and total everything concerning suffering and love. We don' know for sure but we can suppose it's a fitting sort of fretting that takes in beautiful moments, suffering and love. Who can tell?

Well, now, let's see what's happening to Anancy, who's, so far, shaping like a poet-person. He starts to talk with Brother Tiger and Brother Dog. Brother Tiger is a big high thinker. He's talking in a deep subject voice in reply to Anancy: " What to do, Brother Anancy. All you've got to do is wait and see what's going to happen to your wife. You can't jump into her head and direct her traffic the way you want it to go. It's her own way of living the goodness of the garden life; it's her own head and her own traffic. You can't expect to take away her free self from her. Free self is personal property is inside power that nobody can ever hope to take charge of at no time at all."

18

Agreement from Anancy : " True, Brother Tiger. Free self is property is personal is sacred is mos' private."

Brother Dog, who was looking very proud at all the trees around him, looking and thinking how good it is to have lots of real Nature to touch, takes off his tasting eyes from the trees of pleasure and says : " I bow to Anancy to the last word. I can definitely understand why he's having worry head over his wife. Now, take me, for instance, for a test case : I am a straying kind of dog, and if my wife was to get it into her head to follow me everywhere and give me a bitch of a hard time, I would never find my way no place in the garden at all."

Anancy knows that a nod is the correct thing to give at this point, so he puts on a pitiful look and the nod happens like cool breeze.

Brother Dog laps up the pity and starts up a strong supposing : " Now, suppose my wife was to fatigue me with her 'oman-argument and her soft desiring, I would have to live in a spin-and-twist, like when a young dog searching for a tail end. I would have to eat miseries three times a day for seven days a week, including a double share on Sunday day-o'-rest."

Plenty nodding ping-ponging between the two brothers. Brother Tiger is not a nodder. As a brother, he's a reluctant nodder, and Brother Dog and Brother Anancy know that from long time.

So, Brother Dog going on : " Anancy, listen to me and my life. I'm a dog who's very much like a watch dog and a good alarm clock on this marriage harness. I know what is what on the painful subject of the ring thing. I know that a wife is a 'oman with a deep burning inside her, asking for constant sym-pathetic cooling and temperature reading. You see, Anancy : this is how I chew bone on the matter : wife is obedience is company is a sort of bank of love and understanding when things total bright and easy; wife is knowing when to put pressure on 'usban' and when to take it off like poultice; wife is a tricky partner is patience is strategy is a life that must never run jostle with a 'usban' way of moving. That is all I have to say on the raw subject of the gold band."

Brother Tiger, because he hasn't picked up the knack of belly growing and deep growling, just looks at Brother Dog and

19

glances off again in ripe disgust. You see: down at this bottom side of The Beginning, Brother Dog's ideas carry plenty suspicion bad. In fact, most of the other creatures think of Brother Dog as a sort of critic who's always trying his best to spoil other living things creations, because he can't create any beautiful and lasting shapes and sounds for himself. Brother Tiger knows all this about Brother Dog, so Brother Tiger ups and ignores Brother Dog and his top lip talk about Brother Anancy wife.

Well, then, after a touch of hush, Brother Tiger says: "There's a consolation in not expecting too much from others who living round you in the garden, and remember, you can't set up youself like a Boss Man and decide to rub and pencil in people like they are so many names on a list. What I'm trying to say is this: hold on and let what is to happen happen natural like. All right, Anancy?"

Brother Dog rocks himself sideways, a ripe mango on a slender branch, and laughs a stray laugh in Brother Tiger's face. You must understand that Brother Dog is very scornful of things like hoping and waiting and peaceful manners; in fact, he's a war-monger in disguise, something that most critic-persons in The Beginning usual grow to be. They start off a torrent, like promising poet-persons, and somewhere along the ol' life-line, they just dry up like sapling gum in the sun on a dead branch of a mango tree. That's the time when they begin to get on like Brother Dog, hard and Didymus and blind to all the garden sensations and beautiful moments of things in The Beginning.

Hear Anancy: "Brother Tiger an' Brother Dog, you me constan' brothers, don' matter what happen. Any help I want in me personal life, I always come an' visit you down this side of the lan'. Today is a bad day for me, for true. Wife-business is a different sort of business from any other sort of business; it don' make easy. Sometimes I t'ink that maybe worries must be t'ings that I inventin' in The Beginning; I seem the firs' victim of this new t'ing."

Brother Dog nodding two, three times. Brother Tiger watching Brother Dog and disagreeing with the nodding.

Anancy going on: "You know what that wife I got just call me before I come visit you? She ups an' callin' me the conscience of the whole total place. Now, when she sayin' that, I take it an' t'ink quiet an' don' make a move, 'cause how much she meanin', it can't be anyt'ing that nice at all, or else it wouldn' comin' from she; I know so."

Brother Dog nodding again. Brother Tiger playing the passage cute and calm.

" I know so, since she was sayin' it in a turn-up lip way, as if she was smellin' somet'ing ratta-'tink. What I want to know is what I must do with this funny feelin' I feelin' about her an' me. I feelin' some black feelin's about everyt'ing roun' me in The Beginning. I been doin' some heavy t'inkin' lately. The feelin' is like a ton load pressin' down on me face an' chest."

Brother Tiger asking him : " How the feelin' talk to you, Brother Anancy? "

" It don' carry any words with it. It just makin' me jump up like a young banana shoot when night-time come roun'. An' the t'ing that I can't understan' is that the feelin' got a link with the presence of mind of me wife. All the time I keep seein' her figurin' big in the set-up that the feelin' bringin' to me. Then just as I goin' discuss the feelin' with her, she flip-flop over on her side an' accusin' me that I mad no shad an' that she goin' be just as mad as well if I don' stop torturin' her body an' soul. You see, Brother Tiger an' Brother Dog, I t'ink that any bed-respectin' 'usban' should share thoughts, an' for that matter, all deep-down feelin's an' doubts, with the wife he got beside him. An' that is why I turn roun' to talk to her. Maybe there's only one certain t'ing that a wife an' her body an' soul want to share durin' night-time. What you t'ink? "

Brother Dog shaking his head two sides and coming up with : " Same thing I always saying. Wife means a heap of sleepless nights and days of contemplation and brain-pain. If I was like you, Anancy, I would make a change in your policy of treatment of the 'oman you got. I would make her know right away that a man on top and 'oman underneath, like how foot on the ground and head up in the air. 'Usban' is the leader of the wife and her total life and she must follow or drop out of the garden of roses one time."

Listen to Brother Tiger now : " Drop out and go where, Brother Dog? Where she dropping out to? You know something, Anancy : you better leave us and go by youself and think

21

a bit harder about your worries and don' take no Dog advice. Think it out cold and alone."

So, Anancy walks away from his friends, Brother Tiger and Brother Dog, the budding critic-person. Anancy is going along and hanging his head on one side like a lop-sided bunch of bananas in a Doctor Breeze. The most he can do is walk soft and mutter out his worries. All of a sudden, some words start coming from the direction of the serious tree. Anancy is the only audience in sight; that's what it sounds like to him. Pull foot, Anancy! Anancy saying to himself. Better stand up and listen good. Well, then, that is that. The words coming. So, Anancy moving up slow now. Just as he's doing that, he's hearing his wife's voice answering back the voice in the serious tree. Anancy walks on a little and hides himself in the low branch of a sour sop tree. The voices still going on like nobody business, like bees. This is what they sound to Anancy. The wife: " You makin' out that you know all the answers, like drinkin' water out of hand by riverside. I want to find out, too."

This is the second voice. Listen : " I'll tell you. Remember that I was the one who said that if you're not satisfied with your garden plot, you were to come to me and complain? Talking is one thing but doing as I say is another set of parangles. You have to eat this luscious red fruit I have here between this branch. You have to make your 'usban', Brother Anancy, eat some of the said thing. And you must carry the seeds of the luscious red fruit with you everywhere you go. You must carry them; it doesn't matter where you find youself, you must carry them with you and sow them as you go along. Understand? "

A most eager-up answer from Anancy wife, while bowing her head, as if the voice is a grand shrine up in the serious tree. Hear her : " I understan'. All I want from Anancy an' me is a new kind of passion-life. I goin' do anyt'ing you tellin' me, so long as a big change grab we an' blen' we together even like. I mean that."

The other voice : " Good! I like your style. I like your tomorrow thoughts on the subject. You're a very progressive wife. You've got a moving head. No stalling and conserving. I like that plenty. And as for the change of things? Well, you'll get such a definite change that even you'll barely understand what happened to your old born self. I promise you this, as I'm talking to you, here, wrapped round this tree. I promise you progress and change. And when I promise you these two things, you must know that you're the first to get them promised to you, because nobody else has ever asked for them before."

Anancy wife : " I prefer change then progress."

The voice of promise : " Change first then you catch the progress. You're a 'oman with a career spread out in front of you."

Anancy wife : " So, I bite the luscious red fruit, an' then I give Anancy a bite as well? "

The voice of the plan : " No! Not bite. You must eat it. Both of you must have more than a nervous bite. It's really a very sweet first-time experience for the two of you to share together in the garden." The voice stops. Then it says, " As you're alone here, right now, you will have to bite and eat a little piece, as a sort of practice run. I'm sure you'll like it. As you taste the juice, you'll want your 'usban' to try it, too. All right, now, I'm going to pass the luscious red fruit to you. Take it like a new blessing."

Well, Brother Snake (and we must call him that, since he's helping out the first model of a 'oman in distress) starts to make some quick, sliding, up-and-down sounds on the branches of the serious tree. You should see him moving and gliding through all the long leaves, like snake-oil on top of wet Bahama grass. And you should watch him handing the luscious red fruit to Anancy wife. And you should witness how she's positioning herself wide open and taking it from him, with her hands shaking like palpitation.

Brother Snake starts to smile a serpent all over his face. Anancy wife is a quick stick in her naked state. She's taking the fruit and rubbing it on her breasts. She's looking at it and facing a fire experience. She's like seaweed at sunset-time. Brother Snake is feeling the provider of all providers of change and progress, and he's spying hard to see if his customer is obeying him to the last of the garden law. She bites into the luscious red fruit and the juice scatters a fountain all over her face. She swallows the pulp and plenty smiles happen over her eyes. She's moving away from the serious tree. She's going where Brother Anancy standing up and sheltering. She's in a bad trance of sweetness and passion. Her face starts to crease-up into lines and making her look knowing-like. A sudden weight of black clouds settling on her mind. She finds Anancy hiding behind the sour sop tree. Hear her : " I know somet'ing I wouldn' tell a man ! "

Hot neck holding Anancy. Excitement catching him because of what Brother Snake was pumping into her. So, listen to what Anancy saying to her : " How much you know so special? What you got that I don' know a'ready? "

There's a different tone of man-pride in the voice, a sort of hurt-bad man-pride, as if a soft corner lurking somewhere. Man facing 'oman. 'Oman facing man. Things coming to blood. Hear her : " I know somet'ing I wouldn' tell a man ! It bigger than you an' better than you an' more for ever than you can imagine. If you want to know what it is, you got to take a big bite-an'-swallow of this luscious red fruit."

Then Anancy : " You not to make terms like stranger come from foreign, come to trick me with policy an' 'ministration an' development an' rulin' talk an' all that dodge. You must learn to block the temptations of Brother Snake, that tree-habit cold-blooded somet'ing that can't come down on the lan' an' find a livin' like the other animals in The Beginning."

She : " Some live 'igh an' some live low. Brother Snake 'igh."

Anancy : " I suppose he didn' tell you how he used to be a big-time Angel, an' how he slip up bad? "

She : " That is labrish."

Anancy : " Brother Snake slip up so bad that he was the firs' t'ing that ever went through a change. That same fang-mout' used to shine like glass marble, an' then the light just flicker an' blow out."

While Anancy is talking, a mile a minute, his mouth is opening and closing like a swing-to door, and his wife taking away none of her eyes from his mouth. She's taking her time, and just as his mouth clips open again to spout out ol'-time story, she ups and shoves the luscious red fruit straight into it one time. The force of the buck teeth bites off a Big Massa piece and the juice shoots a double spray round his ears. You must try and understand that it was by mistake that Anancy collided with the luscious red fruit, but it's no buck-up, now, the way he's enjoy-

24

ing the taste powerful. Anancy having a real ol'-fashioned back-bite, jaws working a steady clock and showing twelve hot sun, eyes widening and closing cute, nose fanning in and out, slow and easy, and brains having second, third, and maybe even last thoughts on the matter of the luscious red fruit. This is Anancy now: "The bite business is a good t'ing, yes. I didn' know it was so sweet. Nice bad for true. Luscious plenty."

But just as Anancy saying that, something funny happening. He and his wife start a shim sham shaking, like shey-shey, all over the place. The shivering coming on so much that they start looking for some outsize leaf to cover up the shivers with. Then the blue, up-top, begin crackling a ton of pork skin with rain. And the lan' in The Beginning getting grabbed by a giant earthquake. And the serious tree starting to wither-up and look-ing dead. And the animals barking vicious and growling vicious and snarling vicious and hissing vicious. Both faces of Brother Snake laughing loud and proud. Total everything is madness is movement is sound. Anancy and his wife running through the garden. They're just missing the wild animals, as they pass like hurricane leader-wind, up and down. Everything is sizzling is ripping is snorting is slashing swiftness. As Anancy wife tearing arse with speed, so the seeds of the luscious red fruit sprinkling themselves all about the place, as if a Big Massa farmer-man hand doing it. Anancy and his wife running out through the white iron gates and beginning to head out towards a deep forest in front of them. The forest looking and waiting and laughing and black no night and sitting down patient for the two refugees. And still, the seeds going wild in the forest, left, right and centre. Then the two-face voice of Brother Snake starting to shout double loud. Hear it: "Drop all the seeds. I'll reap them later. Every-thing's going silk. You'll get your progress, but what about your change, before that? What sort of change you want? Tell me quick."

But, now, terror-head and panic-heart fixing clamps and battens on Anancy and his wife. They can feel all the wild animals rushing down on them: Lion and Tiger and Dog and Elephant and man-eating Lizard and wild Boar and Boa Con-strictor and Panther and Jaguar and Buffalo, coming fast and breathing low like sin. Anancy and his brain-box stop and think

25

a little bit. They're feeling a new thing running free across face, neck and spine, and right away, the general knowing is that this new thing is fear. The new sensation planting itself in the root of his hair, and he can't like it at all. Hear Anancy to Brother Snake : " Change me an' me wide-eye wife into somet'ing small, I beg you. Change us into anyt'ing that really not too recognizable, anyt'ing that will cause the wild animals to pass by us an' look for fresh meat somewhere else."

Brother Snake was waiting for that : " All right. I'm going to do just that for you and your wife. I'm going to change you into a thing called a spider. But I really can't spare two spiders at the moment. You and your wife will have to be contented to become one total spider and live in that way of oneness until you both die in the same body. Is that all right, Anancy? Tell me quick. The animals catching up with you."

This is Anancy : ' I likin' what you just say, Brother Snake. I likin' it plenty. You just say a good joinin' t'ing. I got to t'ank you for that."

Hear Brother Snake again : " You and your wife ready for the change? Give me the word."

Anancy says : " Change me an' me wife into the oneness of a total spider ! " He and his brains stop sudden and thinking of something else to say to stamp himself cool on Brother Snake. (You see, Anancy catching a learning lesson about the ways of the vast outside brisk.) But, because of the tidal rush of animal sounds, a press button decision grabbing Anancy, and he ups and cuts the thinking short. So, this is Anancy now instead : " Brother Snake, the oneness of a total spider is what I want to be, so that I can spin a web an' catch plenty flies for me wife an' meself, an' that we can live far up in the trees of the forest where the badness of the animals almost can't see us or put foot near us at all. Yes, Brother Snake, change as you want."

And Brother Snake, like how he's so glad that Anancy wife spreading the seeds of the shining politics of change and progress far away into the vast outside, decides to change Anancy and his wife into the oneness of a total spider. Brother Snake is a pattern of coils and magic and tightness, as the power of change comes spurting out of him into Anancy and his wife.

And, I know that you won't believe me when I tell you this, but, from that day until this very hour, this very minute, right here and now, in point of fact, Anancy and his wife actually did become one spider individual person, and the cunning ways Anancy is famous for are the cunning ways of his wife locked way deep down inside him, and the pretty web you see him spinning so is because of the goodness of the poet-person in Anancy own first ol'-time self.

So, if you see a chance web somewhere, don' break it too sharpish and quick without thinking about the poem it might be writing out for you, and think careful how peaceful it would be if we all could really read what it saying in that loving picture-thread writing, like silver fly-way music, before Brother Wind and Sister Rain come and destroy it.

POLITICAL SPIDER

POLITICAL SPIDER

Strange as it may seem, the spider's proper name is Anancy, Brother Anancy in fact, and because he always wore a green coat, his friends, Brother Flea and Sister Leech, called him Hope. Of course, Hope was the extremely private name for Anancy and not really a world name at all.

Well, from as early as early morning-time, all his personal friends called Anancy Hope which, as you know, is a green thing, eternal and all that; and it's for that said same reason that a whole heap of bangarangs was to happen to them.

You think you understand the position?

Now, as a matter of habit, most people can't put out the white light from their minds when they remember that particular morning-time, bright like Big Massa candlelight, when Brother Flea and Sister Leech sat down like double statues, holding on and waiting for Anancy to come and talk about settling all the bad botheration of the jobless spiders, fleas and leeches.

What an Anancy morning it was!

The faces of the spiders, fleas and leeches had plenty uneasiness pricked all over them, like tattoo marks. The spiders, fleas and leeches sat down quiet and strong and ancient like the Boss Man heraldics in the Manor House on North Hill. Everybody was listening to the silence which was yellow like a sort of sickness. Still and all though, yellow silence is a good thing for the thinking out of worries and problems, and it's a hard silence to keep, hard to keep like fast-time in the wilderness. And that was why, like a piece of tight-stretch elastic just begging to snap in two, the quiet started to break up right there and then.

Talk-time. Listen to what one short arse flea saying to his long foot flea-friend : " I bet you anyt'ing that Anancy goin' be late. Funny sort of spider man that. He always doin' all sorts of top hat t'ings as if he face to face with society people. I t'ink he got a bad backra complex, you know."

31

Long foot flea now: " Complainin' can't make rain come. If you talk bad 'bout Anancy, it don' mean to say that we goin' get job an' eat better."

Short arse: " But he always promotin' himself up to the people on North Hill an' I sure this action is a disease that catchin'; it must be a disease, this eye-signallin' an' talkin' with those who come from a different class of ideas an' life."

Hear the answer: " I not backin' down, but you got a point there. That's our trouble. Always, always, Anancy out of reach when we need him bad. He's one green coat spider born to rub up 'gainst high wall an' talk deep talk with a heap of strange people. Sometimes I t'ink that Anancy too much of a political spider for his own spider good an' for our own."

Short arse again: " I don' mind if Anancy wantin' to rub the green coat 'gainst politics an' t'ings like that, because, to tell you the hones' trut', the politics business needin' some green rubbin' off on it. What worryin' me is that Anancy gettin' too deep into the life of those well-off people. You know what I meanin' by that?"

Long foot: " True. Anancy born inquisitive fast. He come with a travellin' eye from a long time back. But, as you know, it can be equal easy t'ing for spider web to get tangle-up with all sorts of outside foolishness."

Short: " An' when that is that, a spider can find himself well on the way to the overseas t'ing called compromise, an' bad starvation an' dark eye boun' to follow bragadap, because a spider can't catch no dinner at all with compromise draggin' him down."

Just as this talking was building up into a mountain of giant sighing and giant breathing and giant statement, one ol'-time spider, with three spangles missing on his right side, decided to chip in and add some ol'-time wisdom. Listen to him talking: " All you young people, with you egg shell still wet, really love to beat up you gum like drum skin rollin' at John Connu time, eh? This no John Connu dance, you know. You always broadcastin' you doubts like red peas on top of ready brown dirt. Grow, you want you doubts to grow, like plantation, yes?"

Long and Short stared at him and gave him blank eye and time.

Ol'-time spider: "You all want to cause big muster an' botheration 'mongst the population down 'ere, eh? Well, let me tell you somet'ing you don' know. You know that Anancy is Hope is a spider is a fighter for everybody. You know that Anancy is a spider is Hope is a green t'ing."

Long and Short nodded like knowing young fleas sitting down and listening with enough rock calm to impress themselves on top of Blue Mountain.

"Well, now," Ol' continuing, "if that is so, true an' 'ones', where, in the name of boundaries an' limits, from Guyana bottom all the way up to me back yard, you expec' Hope to spend his time an' muscle energy, excep' on 'igh places where he can put telescope on our wants an' sufferin'?"

Not a word is a word from Long and Short.

After that piece of wisdom-talking, a crowd gathering round them something big. Ol', not too slow in coming forward, or for that matter, not too shy to hold on to the spot, decided to add one more difficult statement to the first pretty speech. So it going: "The bes' place for Hope is 'mongst the enemy. A spider got to know how the lan' lookin' outside the home web. Livin' with the opposition members is correc' politics. Opposition goin' keep we in power, if you catchin' me meanin'."

The shape of the crowd was moving busy like ants in a fat nest. Everybody was shifting brisk and thick. All sorts of barber shop talk going on with plenty body-fire and hand-crackling. Spiders and fleas and leeches talking about deep high-class subjects like minerals in the ground and red dirt that turning to white in other people country and the quality of Hope and the everlasting example of patience. One light-skinned spider getting up and beginning to spread himself broad and useful, as if he some sort of a new asphalt road or something local and have purpose, and he letting loose plenty words and pictures in the open with a heap of spangle-hands; but if you actually stopping and adding up all the magical things he could be talking about, you would get approx. total nothing at all. According to some spiders in the knowing, he was in training for Park lawyer; so don' mind him.

Then sudden like shock, like ackee without salt fish, or vicky verky, Anancy breezing into the crowd and beginning to fix papers and face, like say he was facing talk in the House of Representatives at crisis-time, like somebody out to prove against him that nothing in 'out of many one'. Anancy standing up and clearing throat hole and popping a delivery in a Tate and Lyle voice. Now, this is a voice he usual put on for the benefit of the sugar starving crowd, as if he talking to a cane-piece gang that holding on to the slack. Hear him now : " Mornin', me brothers an' sisters. I got, 'ere, with me, a master plan which goin' bring us a whole demi-john of contentment of mind, if only you all obey me to the z of it."

" The crowd hangin' on to the z an' wonderin' what coins comin' before it, Anancy," Ol' shouting loud.

" Me countrymen! " Anancy going on, cool as cubes. " Accordin' to me right han' members, all two of them, Brother Flea an' Sister Leech, there's no worl' without rain. They sayin' work scarce an' the fields empty like baby belly six o'clock mornin'-time."

The crowd of spiders, fleas and leeches applauding a small bomb and smiling confidence all over the place.

" All this bad luck," Anancy roaring. " All this goin' on, while, in other parts, wallets an' hand-bags bulgin' with spon-dulix an' green back, like schoolboy pocket with broken plate, string, marble, cotton reel an' such like."

He chuckling a pure parliamentary chuckle. Then he pausing, stamping his spangles for total attention and getting it. He chuckling again. Sudden he looking like a great leader doing himself a Moses.

This is it : " Well, brothers an' sisters, since other people bellies burstin' with good imported food, an' you, me very own, starvin' an' cryin' out for pity, home-made bread an' butter, 'ere an' now, I goin' tell you what to do." Pointing towards North Hill, Anancy making an order now in a torrent voice. " All fleas mus' take up easy residence in all the fat dogs strayin' up yonder; all leeches mus' make house in the sof' underbelly of the horses an' cows heelin' the uplands; an' all spiders mus' hang from the mahogany rafters an' beams holdin' up the great houses on North Hill."

The direction Anancy pointing to is definitely North Hill. And Hope which is green which is Anancy just can't be wrong

34

no how.

Listen to his second-to-last final words: "Move up! All of you mus' move up in life. Foot firs' an' soul after."

And so, Sister Leech fixing a committee in a quick finger-flip. She's getting Brother Flea to head it prompt. She bringing in Short Arse Flea, Long Foot Flea and Ol'-time Spider to serve. And everybody holding a flash sale to the border people and starting to climb the hill to a better life. Some calling it the road to contentment; some saying it be the way from Frome to North Hill, from plantation wages up to man-size income. Spiders, fleas and leeches travelling for days and nights, adding up to half a mango season, and they travelling and obeying Anancy to the z.

So, how this z go? Z is: *All spiders, fleas an' leeches mus' throw way a little of the ol'-time belongin's after every fifty yards of the journey until all the belongin's get dispose of. Secon'ly, after every additional yard or so, a real slight 'ole mus' get sink to open the lan' to the comin' rains. Thirdly, the journey to North Hill mus' 'appen in a slow walk; hurryin' never wise or profitable when Hope handlin' affairs. Fourt'ly, the 'ighes' wall of walls mus' get buil' after the crossin' make into the lan's of the North Hill.*

But that not all. Anancy even had Brother Flea and Sister Leech talking in his own voice and in his own words. Brother Flea: "The rains not fallin' until we return from North Hill content an' fat like John Chineeman. An' when we return, the lan' we put 'ole into goin' be ready to meet we 'alfway with bags of blessin'. An' remember, the 'eavenly mystery of rain, the very special bonus goin' depen' on our fait'ful co-operation with the lan'."

Sister Leech: "You an' me can't fool the rain, an' you an' me can't fool the times we livin' in. Everyt'ing up to we to meet the rain 'alf-way."

The journey lasting fifty more days and nights. By this time so, the lan' fulling up the holes, and all over the place, piles of belongings spreading out like Monday morning washing in a giant back yard. Ol'-time spider, in the mustard wisdom and long-time understanding of things through the years, imagining now that the items trailing out behind him like fishtail, really

35

looking more like dead scrip-scraps : for instance, Willy pennies, cycle-sports betting slips, bottle stoppers and a mixture of smalls with cute value, if you know where to take them for particular uncle treatment.

Well, then, everybody making the crossing and dropping into the grounds of North Hill like Christmas pudding, sweet, thick and sticky. But big 'fraid and shy eye holding on to the new arrivals, and North Hill quiet as Moses baby bottom in bulrush.

But as the time passing, so every man Jack beginning to build the highest wall. Quiet done. Movement is noise is organization is construction going on. Quick and brisk, Babel breaking out, and the wall rising fast no factory smoke.

Anancy, who watching a Nelson-watch a sneaking distance away, straying and staying off there and grinning a jaw-to-jaw grin. The cunning spider eyes like sea-beacons, bright and full of message, like Trafalgar, from the coast side of the brain pan. Click! He standing up on a parapet and shouting leader-man words : " Mc people, I with you. All you wants goin' satisfied bap! Belly bottom goin' full up. Eye done waterin'. Opportunity knockin' pure bangin'. Progress pissin' down. No more Up-class versus Down-class. New groun' under you foot. But careful one t'ing." He stopping short. Nothing pleasing him more than doing that sort of Question Time pausing for effect, as the shoulders hunching and the green coat wrinkling and forming a miracle of folds. He narrowing the eyes and clearing the throat. Hear him : " Nobody mus' venture way from North Hill unless the others ready to drif' back to the Ol' Country. All mus' move as a oneness, like family. Stick together, like plaster, an' work for the V.C.G."

Brother Flea raising trowel and saying : " The Very Common Good."

Anancy nodding. Then he shifting the spangles and rubbing the green coat as if he loving it and himself in one go.

Everybody looking up at him as a sort of celebration column coming to life on the parapet, as if the Anancy self is the coming rain. But no rain coming at all. Only Anancy coming up with : " North Hill you property. One for all. All for one. Out of many one."

36

Stamping spider legs, clapping leech mouths and hissing flea gills making plenty Park bench commotion. And Anancy standing steady like a big-time trans-Atlantic planner and taking all the congratulation noise, saying, without talking it, that he born to it from early o'clock, as if organizing get into him like sleeping, cool and easy. The Anancy face so steady that it looking lasting, marble important, museum for ever. Then he waving for silence and pointing to the green coat. This now: " Hold back the merry-merry an' diges' this. Final words make 'istory, an' 'istory makin' all of we. Work 'ard an' grab. All leave together, like say you comin' out of one single 'oman belly on the lan'. Me name is Anancy is a spider is Hope is a green t'ing."

After he bowing out, spruce-up and down, and smiling and waving off the scene, he coiling himself away tight like ball-father and shooting back to the lan' in the Ol' Country. He flying a streak with plenty pepper corn rent catching fire under him. According to the fever: collecting job to do; job must and bound to get attention quick. But time and rain pouring and lashing natural. The lan' springing up like a young something. It belching benediction. It vomiting vegetables and fruits and things yellow, green and red. The flat earth beginning to look big, and in next to no time at all, it mothering peas and yams and cocoa and bananas and sugar cane. Trees and streams going botanical with a vengeance, and breeze blowing calmness everywhere, and all the tough richness of Up coming down to the Ol' Country.

But Anancy, mister real estate big brains, loving the aloneness, when all the sweetness happening to the lan', and he reaping every drop in sight. Then he bagging the ol' belongings of the spiders, fleas and leeches, and making a brazen sale to Brother Tacuma, the world-famous travelling merchant with a nice nose-bag for extra-large deals. And right after that, Anancy disappearing for the last time from the Ol' Country. If you on the spot at the time and looking at the ace state of the lan' after Anancy done dust it, you would see a proper barren Bible country. Not a thing name thing left behind, not a touch of goodness, not a tree with fruit, not a piece of yam or cocoa or

37

sugar cane. As a matter of story, when story pop, the only thing left was silence and sales echo.

Slap bang, and back, now, to North Hill! Hold on to your brush when I tell you that all the spiders, fleas and leeches even more poverty-up than before the trek. This so, because they don' find no mahogany rafters, no beams, no fat dogs, no soft horses and cows.

Season breeze-blow. Season sun-hot. On and on like that. And the numbers dropping from three million to sixty-three only. Some settle for suicide; some dead from hungry belly and bad dark eye; some cripple flat on the ground when they trying to scale the highest wall they build themselves; and some cry out a bitch wailing and dead from worry-head. But, so with the Ark and so with the nowadays mushrooms, survivors bound to be : Brother Flea and Sister Leech. They humping brick hard experience round with them and still waiting like green fruit ripening.

" So, Short Arse an' Long Foot kick the wicked bucket, eh? " Brother Flea saying.

" An' Ol'-time spider, too," Sister Leech slipping in.

" An' that other one," Brother Flea squinting-hinting. " He doin' it again, sure as sin."

" Who that? " Sister Leech asking.

" Who but Anancy."

" You know somet'ing, Brother Flea? I been t'inkin' that all this is a Job lesson Anancy teachin' we. It a deep somet'ing 'bout we an' 'bout we rockstone struggles on the lan' in the Ol' Country. That so."

" Sister Leech, I been t'inkin' a t'ing, too. Green is a funny colour."

" Green, Brother Flea? " She drifting soft. She not hearing Brother Flea at all. Sudden wappen-bappen, and she screaming a low belly scream, like pain catching up with her.

Then a pause that baffling can't done.

" Lawd," she shouting, " look a pipe."

The stand-pipe in front of them ol' and twist-up. It dripping plenty rhythm.

Brother Flea and Sister Leech take foot and walk over to it

38

and listening to the music coming drip-drip, and Brother Flea looking wide at Sister Leech, because the music saying something the ears hear somewhere else before. A total picture gathering itself from a whole heap of bits and bats. The pieces falling fast as rain and making a wide angle thing in the meantime. Brother Flea and Sister Leech starting to laugh a long hush. And the music talking to them sweet and low. Then both them and the music getting loud and louder, and Brother Flea and Sister Leech laughing a pair of store-bought bellows, on and on, until you would think they going burst open like two overripe jackfruit. The laughing stronger than Samson roaring, and steady as a river running glass to the sea.

Quiet, nuh, and hear me : trust me when I tell you that, if you walk near to your own stand-pipe, you going hear the same music talking to you. And it going be saying the same everywhere : " Is Anancy is a spider is Hope is a green t'ing is politics is Anancy is Anancy is Anancy ! "

ANANCY AND THE GHOST WRESTLERS

ANANCY AND THE GHOST WRESTLERS

I going tell you a story about a spider perhaps not. The spider name Anancy. The story is such a wonder one that not even Anancy himself would want to tell it. And so the mystery of things, believe me.

Well, now, Anancy is a real big spider, the kind with heaps of shoulder muscles, black hairy chest and a night frighten children beard on the chin. Anancy walking is a brute spectacle of all things powerful and massive. He is a miracle of terror. All the same, though, he got a certain sort of high-class dignity together with all the strong presence that most spiders carrying round with them. And this high-class dignity, this big house pride, is also a form of strength. It is a strength in the way that veins and muscles in the arm must be sure signs of stress, strain and strength.

When Anancy walking about the place, he looking like a war memorial, rumbling and tumbling at earthquake time. He the kind of spider who cool and can do plenty things, like swim in river, climb tall mountain and run long race. He come to be a great-time trickster and a giant wrestler as well. Total everybody calling his name and still calling it in a small voice: "Who? Anancy? Man, Anancy is a giant wrestler is a fairground of powers an' muscles. Anancy is a spider is a champion is a strangler is a basinful of big house pride is a real terror is a' ocean of magic with him hands an' foot them! "

So it going that people talking about Anancy in that deep respectful way, all over the place. And when people talk like that, the stories adding up to the building of a house as high as a mountain top, and the top getting covered in total clouds, and even the people themselves losing the ol' touch with the person and thinking of him as out of this world, somewhere far out there in the beyond of Up.

Now, one day, some fat news reaching Anancy, and the news saying that the ghosts from the far country parts thinking of

43

holding a real serious wrestling match; and because Anancy is all Anancy is, he deciding sudden that he going to the far country parts and taking part in the match with the ghosts.

Well, when total everybody in the village hearing what Anancy going do, some of the wrestler friends feeling doubtful and torment-up, some of the political spider friends starting to put bets on him, some deciding to pray plenty for Anancy, and some just shaking head and sighing heaps.

But Anancy, even though everybody considering him a mountain top person, is a man with a mother and a father in the village. He loving them in a great respectful way. But they not liking the wrestling match idea, at all, at all. The mother starting to tell Anancy that it is a foolish business for him to wrestle against ghosts, because ghosts can read a spider mind and they can see clear total everything that a spider going do before he doing it.

All Anancy saying to that is: " One ghos' is a 'undred ghos', an' a 'undred ghos' is only one ghos'. A ghos' is only a ghos' to me." And he still saying it.

But the mother and the father arguing with plenty love in their heart for him. They reminding him of the days when he couldn't even see straight, and of the days when the shadow of a hoe at the slant used to frighten him, and of the days when the smallest noise used to make him draw up all his spider legs under himself and shudder like breadfruit leaf. They trying hard to talk protection into him but all he saying is: " I'm Anancy."

When the mother and the father pleading pretty please, all Anancy doing is stretching out his arms and yawning a wide tired yawn, and going on bored and frighten-up about total nothing in the village or in the world. Later on that said same day, he checking back to the mother, and because she so sad, he whispering some nice spider son words in her ears, and the words making her face lighting up with twinkle eye and merry heart. Then he giving her some corn meal and cassava flour and asking her to make a plate of cakes for him. He rubbing his arms with sweet herbs and he tensing up his muscles. After that, he stepping outside and giving away some juicy mangoes and nuts to the children spiders standing round the hut. Then he shutting the hut door and resting himself tourist cool. Then, after

44

the lay-down, he going to the mother and asking her for the cassava cakes. She looking pale skin and thin face and full of mourning, as if she seeing a funeral standing up in front of her, instead of her own spider son. She clearing her throat and nodding that the cakes not ready yet. Anancy wrinkling up eye-corner and top-lip and getting on suspicious. He puffing and blowing inside like a Mysore bull. So he ups and running down the dirt road to meet his best friend, Brother Tacuma, who always travelling with him wherever he going outside the village. Brother Tacuma is a calm sea, thinking, deep eye sort of spider, constant all the time, walking beside Anancy and smiling plenty consideration for him. This is so much Brother Tacuma and the way he proving himself that he can't be separated from the name 'spider defender'.

So, now, Anancy and Brother Tacuma starting to walk to the far country parts where the ghosts waiting to open the wrestling match. So Anancy and Tacuma walking so they coming into all sorts of darkness in the forest, and a gross of bad sounds and high bird-chirping causing some terrible confusion in the top-half of the trees, and in the bottom-half, the branches and leaves and twigs making some faces of evilness and dead looks and skull-laughter. In fact, there can't be no brightfulness in the forest at all. Big green lizards and scorpions and grass snakes all over the ground, and they going on natural and easy and ugly and hungry like forty days in the wilderness.

When Anancy and Tacuma getting out of the forest, they sagging tired and full of tight muscles so that everything looking like one master blur and hurricane happening. Still, now that Anancy truly reaching the far country parts of the ghosts, he bucking up into a nice piece of good luck. He hearing of a new rule that the ghosts laying down, with clause speckling it like booby egg: " When anybody comin' to wrestle with a ghos' an' the ghos' beat up that body, the custom mus' be for the con-querin' ghos' to carry that body away an' dash the head 'gainst a sharp rockstone which is a special river rockstone fix' up for the purpose."

Anancy considering the news good, in a funny way, because it making him wise and cautious. But he and Brother Tacuma not liking the new rule at all. Stomach turning over flip-flap

45

when they seeing what the ghosts doing to the persons they con-
quering. After watching the bad nastiness happening in front of
him, Anancy, and Tacuma right behind him, spying a small
ghost coiling up nearish to the spot. Listen to how he talking to
Anancy in a nose voice: " So, you two small-time wrestlers
come to the match, eh? I recognise you, Anancy. You still
'mongst the livin' I see. We goin' fix that mistake quick an'
brisk."

To that speechifying Anancy just bowing head and starting
to stretch muscles like foolishness. The small ghost taking that as
Anancy the answer-back wrestler, showing how cool things stay
with him inside. But the small ghost not feeling too good. Hear
him : " Anancy, you t'inkin' that pride wise to have, eh? You
t'inkin' that pride is a good mirror to see youself in proper? Up
an' down this country we breakin' all such mirrors."

After a little foot-shifting, throat-clearing, flexing and hustling
here and there, things really looking like business. Anancy starting to fight now. Even though broad daylight everywhere, the
silence surrounding everything and everybody resembling the
silence inside a Sunday morning. The first ghost contestant is a
tall ghost with hands and feet like ol'-time electric fan, actually
going on mad and circular like so. The ghost tough like croco-
dile skin and stiff like ice. And because the stiffness bringing ice,
the ghost slippery out of this world. But Anancy is a mover
can't done, moving up and down like a jack-in-the-box in trance,
diving into the ghost, twisting him up and plaiting him round
like straw, and before you could say Jack Mandora, dropping
him light like roll-up silver paper. After that, Anancy doing
nothing else but grabbing the mash-up ghost and dashing him
down on the river rockstone fix up for the purpose. As soon as
the ghost vaps up 'gainst the rockstone, he splintering fine no
icing sugar, and just as white as that.

Brother Tacuma starting to feel an ace proud feeling walking
foot 'cross the physog for Anancy and for what he carrying on.
Tacuma just quinting at Anancy and smiling a brother smile
at him.

Then another ghost coming out and playing facety and sizing
up to Anancy with plenty hot breathing, territory insults and
wild nose talking. This ghost showing four heads, a big-time

46

central one with three other sudden ones sitting sub off it. But Anancy checking cute bad, heeling and balling up and down the wrestling ring and catching a spin bright as a spinning ol' two-and-six piece. When he revolving so, the four-headed ghost getting dizzy and all the eight eyes turning over and jumbling up like john crow bead. Anancy stepping heavy and stepping fetchit and dancing round, Cassius back o' Ali, until, ting-a-ling, the four heads drop off, vup, vup, vup, vup. When they connect with the ground, they roll away in four which-way 'cross the ring, and the body crumpling up like dry grass.

Well, now, after that pretty-pretty victory, another ghost walking into the contest. This one carrying eight heads, and it thinking eight times faster than Anancy and the one head he got there. But already Anancy ready, and according to science, he throwing a bitch lock round the ghost neck. And as Anancy spannering, crick, the eight heads drop off cold.

Then Anancy grabbing the next ghost who having ten heads, and he wrapping him up as if nothing don't even go so. He doing the same with the twelve-headed one and the fourteen-headed one and the sixteen-headed one and the eighteen-headed one and the twenty-headed one. You not going to believe me when I tell you that the heads rolling all over the lan' like red garden cabbage, and the eyes blinking a last look-see, white, black and red. The ground totalling a swarm of ghost spare parts.

By this time so, Anancy knowing that he causing the ghost territory a lot of worry head. And like how logic brains have a way of borning logic brains, which meaning that the ghosts who promote the wrestling match deciding to hold a Ghosts United Conference same time, that is what happening. Big defeat meeting of nose accents going on in deep session. After they talk plenty summit, they find the answer to the Anancy problem, and this is the final solution : " Anancy will 'ave one las' fight. An' this time, he mus' fight him own spirit."

Imagine that class of mystery, now ! Anancy fighting Anancy. Yet, that is the natural confusion of things, believe me, right where you sitting down. Body 'gainst spirit, spirit 'gainst body, but, at least, this going be one spirit with only one head. Both of them standing up and facing each other, Anancy body and

47

blood fronting Anancy spirit and soul. As they looking square, the eyes making four formal like.

All the total royal-catching, promoting ghosts holding a long, low-breathing commission quiet, and thinking even-Stephen and quits and revenge. The day name day come.

Anancy spirit drilling through Anancy body, and Anancy feeling a raw X-ray burning him. On top of that, a fast crumpling mish-mash setting up in muscle and bone. Anyway, after brain and soul ping-ponging some message and signal, the spirit flashing a lightning bolt straight through the body and lashing it 'gainst the rockstone. The body splintering into pure confetti.

Listen all the ghosts now: " Ai-yi-yi! At las' it come to pass. At las' it dey. Who ever hearin' say anybody can fight 'gainst him own life an' get 'way wit' it? Serve him right. Proudful an' stupid arse spider wrestler."

Slap after that mixture, the chief ghost walking foot into a real thick clump of bush-john, picking some berries off the bush-john trees, and squeezing the juice into the eyes of all the dead ghosts. Then they jumping up and beginning a sweet piece of living again and talking through them ol'-time nose voices.

Brother Tacuma watching the chief ghost restorer and deciding to do everything he seeing him doing. And so, Tacuma ups into the real thick clump of bush-john and picking some berries off it and squeezing the juice into Anancy right eye, then, into the left one. Sudden no harbour breeze, Anancy coming back to life like he hearing say taxes gone. He fulling out to a normal spider self, cool. Yet, even though he getting the feeling of the living body again, he prickling angry bad and starting to grumble and quarrel with the Anancy spirit for being a proper Judas person to him. He talking man to spirit, straight no chalk line, and saying how he hating the bitching back-bite it do to the Anancy body. And so, the row revving on for a long, horse-plantain time.

When the ghosts returning to find Anancy and to pick up the spider pieces and eat them for supper, they not seeing the Anancy food wreck at all. But they hearing him far off. They hooking up with him, and tapping him swearing and shouting in the distance and quarrelling with the break-faith spirit and running way as fast as fart from the far country parts. So, the ghosts

48

deciding to chase and capture them flying supper. Mad races, now. Ghosts catching up. Speeding is pure blue bird and power house between them. Anancy and Tacuma getting nearish home. Ghosts opening out to a bigger speed, and forest making *mucho* celebrating noise like hurricane breeze-blow. Anancy and Tacuma turning the last corner and heading for the door leading into Anancy mother hut. Ghosts coming, now, flying low like gingy-fly madness and cursing red pepper. Then Anancy, from nowhere, starting to feel weak, as total courage and green oozing out of him same so. The water sensation biting into the high speeding and slowing it down. But as the slowing down coming to facts, badambam, something bursting deep down inside Anancy belly. Anancy spirit, who having this big disagreement with Anancy body, declaring to show that he not no Judas person at all. So, the spirit (one-time conqueror and *only* conqueror of Anancy) shooting out of Anancy sweating body and eating Anancy mother cassava cakes and licking lips loud and beginning to tackle the swarming ghosts. The spirit performing some wicked wrestling tricks that the ghosts never read about anywhere. And after the count of twelve, most of the ghosts crying out enough pain-pang and turning round the other way and tearing backside back to the far country parts; all the same, a few of them not moving too good because they collecting blows and battering and splintering.

As soon as the ghosts not no more, Anancy spirit making a real loving come-back into Anancy body with a pretty cassava satisfaction broadcasting calm 'cross the muscles, and, as that happening, a joyful heaven-come-down-to-earth smile spreading itself all over Anancy face. Brother Tacuma hawk eyeing the joyful heaven-come-down-to-earth smile over Anancy face, and he relaxing and feeling a swelling puffing-up inside himself.

And, now, in front of him, Anancy mother and a big enamel plate of cassava cakes, Anancy testifying and making the village know that a person only strong for true, at home or in the far country parts, after that person spirit prove him straight and narrow in the thick of things.

49

ANANCY, THE SWEET LOVE-POWDER MERCHANT

ANANCY, THE SWEET LOVE-POWDER MERCHANT

Time was in Mount Calm village, when white rum, dominoes and a clay pipe could be total more than all the waga-waga spending money you could earn in town. A big gill of whites in two, a photo-frame hitch proper in a domino game and a tobacco-up clay pipe would be all in all that any conscionable person would want to happen to him on the lan' in Mount Calm. Those days things prospering hands down, and peace was peace. Mount Calm was a ground lizard in sunshine: Brother Baker losing little bit of pence to old Brother Cane Cutter; Brother Bar Owner to Brother Tailor Man; even Bird Patoo Owl to Bird Grass Quit; all this, until Brother Anancy, the travelling merchant spider, arriving with a gripful of heavenly oddments, including some first-class packets with SWEET LOVE-POWDER write up 'cross them.

Not too long and Anancy getting a bitch reputation as a master domino player; the news take foot and spreading through the village like wild fire; and even going in front of this is the labrish about the stuff he intending to spider hawk round Mount Calm; this reaching everybody fast no wasp. Now, Sister Sally, a bad-off sex wife, 'cause of her husband, Brother Benjamin, and the domino gambling and white rum drinking he for ever going in for, deciding to consult Brother Anancy. And so, the consultation talking happening and Anancy professional down to him toe-nail. He finishing off with the following subtle-up operation: hear him: " Firs'ly, cut down on the starch conten' in the ol' man diet; you know the sort o' t'ing I mean; don' bother serve yam or yampie, no cassava, no breadfruit, no corn-meal dumplin'. Today, day, I mean, you mus' start. Secon'ly, every evenin' you mus' give him a luscious egg custard, wit' all the nutmeg sprinkle 'pon top o' the nice cream. Now, wit' every time you feed him, you mus' sprinkle lavish some o' the miracle stay-wit'-me-an'-love-me-for-ever powder I goin' prescribe an' give you."

Sister Sally and Anancy facing each other and them eyes making four serious, and as if she under Brother Satan control, she bowing her head in a pretty please, yes. As Anancy handing over the love stuff with one hand, he collecting two mash-up ten shilling notes with the other, and if he could produce a third hand, it would've been straight up Sally dress taking a feel. Sister Sally shuffling off muttering the instructions to her new hopeful sex self; she trusting bad.

So, the days going on. It was most a total hour after the third righteous dinner of brown rice, red peas, ox tongue and egg custard that Sister Sally husband, Brother Benjamin, fall down sick bap, and as a natural consequence following, a natural spider one at that, Brother Benjamin had was to miss the usual late night doings at Brother Joshua tavern. This was the first correct broadcast proof of Anancy cute magical powers. He was going to be, at last, the fixer all Mount Calm wives waiting for. Brother Benjamin groans sounding ocean long and concrete in everybody ears-hole. He tossing and soldier turning and twisting. In the groaning hours he dreaming nothing but the sessions he missing down the tavern. After two, three days nursing Brother Benjamin, Sister Sally sure as salt that Anancy bound to be the spider saviour come to all Mount Calm woman with husband-worries and crosses to bear, and she making plenty advert about Anancy powders to all her gossipful friend them. Sister Ma Jenkins telling Sister Stephanie Walters, and Little Sister Hilda begging Sister Lue and Sister Georgina to do as Sister Matty and herself doing. They saying like radio that Anancy is the man with a plan, the right fixer in the van.

A quick, brisk week and Mount Calm village was most total without man life. All the woman them in a calico quiet, forming into clump, one, two and three, and labrishing about the latest case of stay home. The wife-chuckles slipping out like cherry seed with bands of hand movements concerning some magic-up husband behaviour in bed the night before. Small detail chasing small detail like camera taking picture. All the same though, the only sort of Mount Calm life in the village streets, apart from the happy, wicked woman say-say, would be the children them playing : some with them vomiting father domino pieces, some with broke-up clay pipes, some with chip-up white rum glasses, and some with nothing at all but them own top note voice and the sing-song mento singing the washer woman them carrying on at the river side. You should hear how they celebrating in round rockstone chorus, most parson perfect: " Abide at 'ome wit' me for ever an' ever " and, as per usual, as a last woman dig in ribs, Sister Stephanie Walters soloing with : " Man no' wise, 'cause 'oman smarter than man any time o' night, don' even care if she done jus' drop her drawers an' her foot wide open for the t'ing."

Not a domino banging pretty anywhere at all. Not a smell of white rum either. Not a bad behaviour is a bad behaviour. Night time and Mount Calm village seeming another out of this world set-up. Through the open window blinds in the lean-to tenement husband vomiting loud can't done, like rain falling on zinc. The poor man them squirming sick in bed with them satisfied wife them dancing Anancy attendance and feeling secure as peas in pod. All looking neat, most like marriage bliss, with the Mount Calm wife population, and the same thing with Brother Anancy, the travelling merchant with too much blasted difference to mention. You should catch a listen and hear him spider boasting like schoolboy down the gully at evening time : " I know I could fix the village, Now I goin' be a rotten rich spider personality in the *Gleaner* at las'. Never 'fore now so much 'usban' take so much fool-fool powder in the name o' so much love to rass! An' the wife them? They stupid bad. Man, you can sam people easy no cheese in the country bush, eh? What a bitch! " Brother Anancy, like most just-arrive grabalicious samfie-man, drinking more than one spider fair share of whites, and people seeing him as he spangle staggering round the village at all sort of unclockable hours. With one spider-pound for every love packet he selling, he can afford to rock like blind eye boat for months. He making extra spider-demands on four, five, six of the wife believers, explaining that the request is part of the working of the power powder. Listen him : " If when I ask you for a piece o' pussy, you goin' say no, then I can't say that I sure that all goin' go good at 'ome. You mus' understan' that even the 'oly Church Law own sayin' is that *a little sweetness given always brinin' back blessin' o' sweetness on the giver.* Right? "

55

So, it go that one morning, after enjoying a whole night of sweet thief pussy, that he staggering through the market place and get stop by an early morning prospective customer. She telling him that she waiting and wanting the usual love packet. He telling her to hold on to the slack. He go and come back spider eager and she dropping a pound in the palm and walking on quiet-like. Brother Anancy staring hungry at the new customer. She impressing him a whole heap, because of her definite outside Mount Calm manners and general body looks. She white bad, if you catch the meaning.

Anancy asking Sister Stephanie Walters, who standing nearish to the happening : " Who that 'oman that jus' buy the packet off me? "

And Sister Stephanie : " She be the local M.O. wife, a nice lady who jus' come from foreign." Then she adding some more words : " She come from over yonder col' fog-up there'll always be an Englan'."

Brother Anancy chuckling and saying soft : " Look, Lawdie Missa Claudie! You mean to say that I catch she an' all? I wonder if Parson wife goin' patronise me nex'? This Mount Calm is a real firs' class, A-1 Promise Lan' for all climbin' spider travellers like me so. Fancy that. Firs', I fool the wife them, an' then, the Medical Officer missis. Cool breeze! "

Unbeknownst to Brother Anancy, the M.O. wife long time suspecting him and the wonder love powders, and only doing what she did plan between her Englan' self and her Englan' M.O. husband. The purchase was a cute operation to pretty flatter Brother Anancy. This kind of foreign plotting behaviour, she reasoning, going put some fine salt on the bird own bottom feather. After all said and done, it clever best to have the spider culprit hanging round a little longer until the Englan' net set proper. And she planning right. Poor Brother Anancy swallowing the bait, claw, rope and rockstone, the total vanity length of it.

Time and the Englan' M.O. finding that the love powders causing the spread of vomiting sickness in the village. As soon as the tests finish vap and the test tube answering back positive, the M.O. reporting the germ findings to the Englan' Parson who announcing the news at the nine-thirty Communion Mass that

56

a most serious fraud been perpetrate in the village midst, we can sure as fate; that everybody been most blind in going straight into the web of the powders peddling jinnal from the city.

As hot word saying that the Englan' exposure reaching the husbands, a shock tearing arse in the ol'-time hush-hush. The husbands, in them first-time-on pyjamas and night shirt, grabbing hoe, machete, fork, spade and any digging thing at hand and going after Anancy. The Sunday Service calm, Communion and all that, breaking up like bread into a bangarangs of pyjama and night shirt spectacle. All the women and children staying inside under lock and key. Sister Stephanie Walters and Sister Mammie Jenkins managing to woman-spy on the happenings by climbing up to the fan-light top. Sister Mammie Jenkins stifling a belly cry as she seeing her husband Brother Jonathan sprinting off like Cocoa Brown and waving machete like Olympics madness. And there was total more to see. The three Brother Martin brothers bringing out horses; Brother Timothy Small carrying a long cow cod and cracking ring-master as he joining the crowd; and the blacksmith, Sister Sally husband, Brother Benjamin, gradual-like dragging a wide-out net and swinging ten inch of black, crack-skull iron pipe.

All ready arrange-up and thing, and the search party licking out like grass snake. After it rounding the Clock Tower, everybody bursting with *Onward, Christian Soldiers!* The party tramping about plenty hundred yards when it meeting up with two pale horse riders clopping from the opposite way. As the two riders getting nearish to the party, the husbands recognising them as the Englan' M.O. and the Englan' Parson. The message that they bringing with them sad bad no rass. 'Nough disappointment trickling itself through the husbands fast. The Parson telling them how Brother Anancy escape on a Kingston train just about the time when he himself announcing the germ findings of the M.O. at Communion. The husbands looking at one another and then back at the Parson; then they breaking into a big dash for the houses. Few of them swearing black is white and shouting set-hand.

But, with Anancy gone like lightning, by the next night, Mount Calm village echoing a fairground with hard knocks from hitching dominoes and white rum talk, mostly about

57

Anancy and the deceiving powders and pussy power. The oldest husbands grouping together tight as cabbage leaf and biting into the dents on the clap mouth clay pipe them. Ol' Brother Papa Paul nodding to Brother Cousin Jabez knowing-like, as total all of them pondering the spider ways of the big city and white brains.

Mount Calm is one country village that Anancy can't sam again, Englan' or no Englan'.

VIETNAM ANANCY AND THE BLACK TULIP

VIETNAM ANANCY AND THE
BLACK TULIP

Anancy was a black spider walking the streets a bitch time, in all about some two, three, four months, searching for a spider job. Every day-time, the pavement them sprawling before him like gallows plank. Anancy having thoughts wandering up and down a stream of black ants on a brick wall in the harbour. The straight up and down moves sparking off bands of breadfruit eyes in the front of the spider head. That going on and Anancy thinking of kicking plenty stones when no stones to kick anywhere at all. He shoving one arm, quick and brisk, into coat pocket and pretty plucking out a so-so make-believe cigarette, and with a make-believe match, setting a make-believe fire under the smoke end. Then he making a make-believe blow-out in the face of a batter-up capstan by the street corner. The blow-out is a propaganda thing, a proper imagine business, napalm coil of smoke wrapping Anancy physog, like say how the real puff did wrap it some time back in a swamp. But just as he doing all this inside rummaging in the brain pan, sudden as a flick-flack wrist flick, he seeing the butt-end of a cigarette curling cute in a rum advert ashtray not too far from the spot. He beginning to ease up the hold he got on the make-believe cigarette, hiding it from the dream one, with a sort of fast finger flip he using all the time to keep up with the hot foot of the inside head game he playing since Vietnam. He shuffle strolling and chuckling bad because he get catch by the said tricks he inventing. So, he walking on, head bending down, foot kicking, or with a whole lung case of smoke just dreaming out of him in a ring easy blow-out. The play was either one or the other or all three: head bending down with foot kicking or foot kicking with a whole lung case of smoke just dreaming out of him or head bending down alone or foot kicking alone or a whole lung case of smoke alone or head bending down, foot kicking with a whole lung case of smoke just dreaming out of him in a ring easy blow-out. So the mad-up world of Anancy stay, as he walking through the south-west gate of the Park. This was the brain-poverty or brain-riches, any way you want it, while he getting nearish the first bed of tulips.

Now, Anancy, touching close thirty, did have, what was common consideration, a total life for a young black spider: he did fight plenty spider war overseas for a mothering or uncling, distant, cold-over country; marrieding at twenty and losing the missis in a train-crash, a real funny sort of ordain train-crash; and now, as he returning to spider civilian life, with a proper civvy swagger, he finding himself without Uncle and without a rass. He obtaining a force-ripe pension from the Spiderment for a spangles disability cause by a terror napalm burn-out. And last thing: as he walking and making believe, he got the one consolation to be one of the world-time spider-unemploy. He constituting a pasero under stress and strain, feeling some horror and blood events, and even with that so, he after-War settling down right slap inside the narrow life and knocking soft. But Anancy having a Park sensation now. He stopping beside a tulip bed. Never a tulip as magic pretty plenty as the one that swaying a dance 'nough inches over the rest of them in the Park. Anancy feeling a magnet pulling him to this particular tulip. It showing a real out of this world colour. It looking *black,* a real A-1 oily black, standing up and hitting the other tulip them with a definite stabbing dagger defiance. Three Dagger Rum is foolishness to it! Anancy staring at it, contemplation-self. Then, slow, in a far-off way, he puss-moistening the spider lips, and he saying to himself in a cute whisper: " A *black* tulip? Funny." The pictures in Anancy head running some wild pumpkin, criss-crossing giddy no gig, as he catching a comparison with other black things he knowing: sure as sin, black cat and black dog; most usual, black hat and black car; even black sheep; but, no, this tulip black bad, and it not no cat, no dog, no hat, no car, and not no sheep, for that matter.

Like you say two set of dog on heat, two spider couple them rustling so walking past Anancy, and talking cool concerning the sands at a top hat resort by the coast. One spider man throwing a quick glance down on Anancy shoes, tatter-up terrible in a pout and frill-lip way round the welts, and the man giving law for pea soup plus a top hat snob remark, far from the bathing cove topic, as foreign as fart. Anancy sort of half-hearing the tittering of the top hat spider women them, and starting to follow them gaze straight down. He tracing it down to him own shoes. He smiling a lock purse smile, as he noticing that the shoes spider black.

Some two weeks and little bit after that happening, Anancy coming every day to catch a look at the black tulip. It standing straight up like a slim body. It seeming a proud thing and looking stylish and woman individual, like say it owning the lan' under it, don' matter it only a small piece of dirt and such. So the days passing like speed merchant and he coming and standing statue before it, gazing adoration down at the thing, as if it got him under some sort of obeah or what. Now and then, he thinking of black cat and black dog or black hat or black car, and even black sheep. Other out and out times, he thinking of all five, two pairing off and meeting up with the others like funny germs, head and tail, under microscope. Then sudden thing, he not thinking no more of the dream objects them, and he even throwing way the secret making believe dream-game of smoking and stone-kicking scoring tactics and all so. Plain and simple like, something else taking them place.

Well, now, Monday come. That said same morning, Anancy making a giant rush out of the room and muttering some soft life mutterings. Then he whispering : " Black tulip." He calling it 'nough times and making a beeline for the Park. When he get on spot, he starting to stretch out a spangle hand, thinking he going touch the black tulip sweet and light. But some powers grabbing him with a machine dynamo and causing him to hold on to the smoothness of the woman stem. The tension gone so giant high up that the stem breaking crips in the fever hold he holding it with, which is a proper terror hold. He swinging a quick look round him and then he shoving the broke neck tulip inside him trouser pocket on the right hand side. So, now, he standing sharp and muscle vibrating, like he in Vietnam bush. He saying to himself to wait 'til he ready calm to move off with certain heart and movement, like a spider person who don' do nothing cruel or killing sort of. From the Vietnam days, he knowing for a fact that he can't do it no other way. The certainty feeling coming fast. He moving off a real spider person, con-

63

science easy and cool U.S. breeze. He walking to the furnish room and making out to himself that he sporting a new merry-merry deep down. He spider crossing most of the street them without the usual look right, look left. Nearish the house, he breaking out in a tin whistle whistling. He 'membering a tune the soldier boy them singing under big 'fraid in Vietnam. He whistling sugar and offering up the tune to the black tulip. He feeling a good feeling of ownership. He get home in the same mood and fixing up every man jack in the room to say welcome and howdy to the black tulip. It standing tender and fresh doctor morning wind, nice no young gal, in a jam jar, half with cold pipe water, on a side table. Anancy turning and twisting the bottom of the jam jar in a heap of different viewing angle. Twice a day, he taking love and deciding what to do next for the black tulip, so it be comfortable and make a beautiful picture. He venturing some hard discussion business in the head, as to which fitting plan he going take up to see that all is love and contentment. He even leaving a window up at night so a nice breeze can blow freshness over the black tulip face.

Since the last day in the Park, and after a gradual brain-working action, he convincing himself strong that the earth can't be no happy place for the beautifulness of the black tulip, and, as 'cording to him, he certain that the room is the Garden of Eden own self. He thinking up scenes : earthworm them with picks attacking; starchy dirt sucking the root them dry; bad weather battering the body; or a boy pickney ball bruising the face. Anancy having some cute sensation coming to him. He imagining a few bread crumbs can't do no harm, if he slip them into the jam jar. He taking plenty long walks and carrying the black tulip, warm inside the spider shirt he got on. He tin-whistling and singing one or two Vietnam *mento*.

So what you think happen? After one of the long walks, when he chipping back to the room, he noticing the flesh on the black tulip half-slice way from the stalk. The shock shake him 1692, and when it wear off natural 'nough, he give up the long walks as a bad bargain. Instead of the foot works them, for hours he sitting and humming pure Vietnam or reciting spider poetry. All this substitution ending up with a slight amount of worry-head and anxious heart. At the end of that said week,

64

Anancy spidering out of bed one morning to find that the black tulip dead like rockstone. It looking separate and crumple-up like common something. Anancy staring panic at the jam jar and redness trickling down the spider spine. He scrambling the sadness round the room and feeling a tall building toppling deep down inside himself. As he dragging on the spider shirt, he 'membering that he don' do no ' smoking ' for weeks on end. Sudden sparks and he missing the secret knowing-game. He missing it but he smiling a most knowing smile to himself. So he walking to the room door. While he doing that, he eyeing the room door key and the front door street key, lying on the side table beside the single bed. He going past the side table, without as much as batting eye on the keys or wanting to take them up, out to the corridor, through the front door, and, baps, in to easy street.

Story go that the people them last seeing Anancy stepping heavy and slow nearish the deep sea water down by the Pier, with the spider head bending down, foot kicking, or with a whole lung case of smoke just dreaming out of him in a ring easy blow-out. The play was either one or the other or all three : head bending down with foot kicking or foot kicking with a whole lung case of smoke just dreaming out of him or head bending down alone or foot kicking alone or a whole lung case of smoke alone or head bending down, foot kicking with a whole lung case of smoke just dreaming out of him in a ring easy blow-out.

65

ANANCY, THE SPIDER PREACHER

ANANCY, THE SPIDER PREACHER

Brother Oversea the name I got, and most people calling me that without even cracking them mouth corner with a smile. Anyway, I got a story to tell you about Brother Anancy. The story got to be the sort of story that going make you think forty time, sick in stomach, sick in heart.

Brother Anancy living in the hills back of beyon' Hardware Gap, a longish way from the spot where the giant Tamarind standing statue one time. Anancy managing to spider build a wattle-and-daub and plant a few small crops. With next to no farmer spider necessaries at all, Anancy spending nearish to thirty years lock up inside Heaven Corner. This name you mustn't take for joke; it got a bitch underneath meaning round it and such like. So, now, this Heaven Corner, to camera eye tourist, would be most ugly for true; but, for Anancy self, it meaning sweet home with the pretty embroidery and thing. Take the wattle-and-daub: it standing in a clearing bake by Brother Sunlight and pat down longish hours 'til it hard and looking like Brother Macadam twin. Over the wattle-and-daub entrance hanging some dry entrails of two, three brother animal or sister bird or others. The dirt yard flooring in the inside seeming double hard than the outside. Inside got three low stool, and I wondering why Anancy bothering with so much stool since he don' got any visitors and don' seem to want none. A mad bawl-and-grin-and-bear-it skull-and-crossbones shining out bright from the crevice in the far right hand corner nearish the door way. On a table, dead centre in the wattle-and-daub, resting plenty sister bird feather and heaps of dung. The feather them smelling a dirty creamish colour. On top a lean-to contrivance-thing, the spider people in the region calling a beje bed, a few nasty sheet of discoloured back paper laying down mash up. The bed panelling got some faint sort of nail scratching, like ghost message. Top these, 'nough bottles hanging. First glance,

69

they looking to be medicine flasks, but when you catch a second glimpse, you discovering that they nothing but throw-way ginger ale bottles, two dozen of them, dangling on inch nails, slanting into a bit of mahogany boarding-up. Some 'nough of them full up with water; some 'nough empty. The others them having a fleshy substance floating round in a bluish, greenish or pinkish water. I bending over the bed for a personal look-see. I seeing that the fleshy bits could be scrips-scraps of snails, lizards, caterpillars and even wild run-'bout mushrooms. Next thing was a bookstand full up with old-time magazines; then three fat Bible under the bookstand hiding half cover with a canvas matting. The Bible them have three particular distinct colours : one blue, the other green, and the third pink.

Sudden no lightning, I get distract by a quick sound tinkling so going on somewhere. I looking up and I witnessing the bottles catching a sweet sway in a wind blowing through the wattle-and-daub. I turning to the door now. I hearing a voice.

" Haul you arse out! I don' want nobody 'ere. I didn' ask for no company."

Spider man, Anancy self. He tall and muscle-up thick. He looking sixty or so. The spider body bearing like officer soldier and meaning pure business. Two spangle arms hanging heavy crook stick from the hairy shoulders, broad as bitch, mirror shining with sweat and plenty veins running up and down and crossways. He wearing only a khaki short pants and the spangle legs them contour-up with dry mud. The foot them brown like knot wood.

I looking at him face. The eyes glaring out 'nough fire, mark-up with scatter shot, and wild like madness.

" Get out! " he saying again, changing up the words.

I standing steady statue. Me hand them itching a tickling feeling down the wrists. They clammy no clammy cherry. I wanting to say something, any Gawd thing, but I couldn't raise a speak at all. I walking outside the wattle-and-daub, counting the footsteps, one, two, in a personal fever. As I passing him, he spit kaa-tu !

I saying, " I sorry, man. I was wanderin' roun', an' I see you place. I decide to stop an' make you 'quaintance. So it go." I hoping to tongue draw him little bit to start up a talking betwixt and between. 'Nough fake nerves catching me and making the temperature drop. I not too frighten now at all. I facing him. He kind of looking sort of harmless, like somebody draw him teeth. The last piece of protest sound like short pants pickney own, as though something get snatch way from him and gone to next door neighbour. He just standing up and not moving one striking thing, not a foot, not a hand, not a finger. Then he tilting him head up so and giving out a wake dead moaning. It bellowing out, then tapering off like fee-fee. Then he making a few decorating sign in the air, chopping it up with him hands, and after that, he running into the wattle-and-daub. Some footprint them, and that's all left to show he been actual standing up before me. I peep into the wattle-and-daub, but Anancy not there. I walk way baffle and disappoint 'nough a'ready.

Later that night down the village, I asking pretty please concerning Heaven Corner. I ask Brother Tacuma, the Area father, about Brother Anancy, but all I getting back is some Didymus warning not to go up to Heaven Corner again.

Early before sun-up next day, I decide to walk foot to the Area township and talk with Brother Mongoose, Brother Patoo and a few of the washerwoman sisters. The hot breathing they informing me with almost total, word repeating word, the same as Brother Tacuma own the night before. Then they open up, when they seeing that I not satisfy with the hickory they talking. They saying that Anancy come to the Area over forty year ago now. That time so, he real slim. He a young city spider with usual city manners and city looks and city thing. He 'nough boasify and reckless and dropping style 'pon everybody round the place. After maybe a month, the Anancy luck starting to salt and change from good to bad to worser. Some sort of way, he not holding the villagers with him spider city magic no more. Story go that be beginning one bright Sunday morning time to keep the first prayer meeting in the Square. He telling total everybody that the Spidering Church misleading them too much miles from the deep truth of things. As 'cording to Brother Patoo, Anancy fix up himself neat middle of the Square and shouting : " Come, follow me. Lef' the Church alone. Lef' it for sinners

71

who t'ink they really sinnin' in trut'. F'them religion don' belong to we. You ever see the colour o' them pictures? You ever notice the Lawd face? I's people like you an' me paint it, you know. An' that wrong, deceitful bad. No morals into it, I tell you. Lef' now an' follow me an' I goin' explain everyt'ing to you. Come now ! "

The anti-Spidering-Church following grow fast like love bush. The Anancy opposition to the Spidering Church giving the local spider missionary them a heap of worry-head. They trying to battle off the terror heresy, but Anancy putting him head down like bull and wrestling with them toe to toe like a master anti-force. But he not to have him way so easy. The Spidering Church asking the Spidering Police to assist them, and together like they telling Anancy not to hold no more public anti-meetings. The following, as mirror consequence, coming larger and swelling everlasting. Anancy preaching in the hills and caves and some-times right slap in the deserted cane field them. After three months of crafty hiding out and dodging, a rumour saying that he performing plenty masterful healing service outside the village. And, on top of that, he preaching some hard lines. The substance go so : first, the Lawd is not no overseas man and spirit at all 'cause He like Anancy self, flesh and blood and natural; second, heaven don' exist, and hell right yah so 'pon earth; third, man bad no sore; fourth, Gawd cute.

Next, I meeting up with Sister Granma Ethel. Her story not agreeing, dot-i and cross-t, with the rest of the story them. She saying that Anancy head himself straight into a bad sin, when he call down all the vengeance curse of heaven and hell on the join hand office of the Spidering Church and the Spidering Police, baps up to the point where them family get include. This all-in curse affect Anancy following bad. Sister Granma Ethel saying that they wouldn't lef' Anancy if only he did rebuke them soft with a Bible rebuking, but like how he curse them so strong, it turn the following anti-him. And then Anancy meetings drop off to nothing. Sister Granma Ethel, who been a staunch trust-believer, swearing blind to this. She saying that Anancy try hard holding the following but not a hold was a hold. Whenever he calling service only boy and gal pickney them gathering

72

round him, and them intentions farish from total honourable, as Sister Granma Ethel reminding me. And as soon as Anancy starting to spider preach, the pickney them forming a big circle round him and staying quiet. Then at a pre-arrange time, they taking out them slingshot them and David him a target hard with a heap of sharp river rockstone. This happening a few instance, and one time, when he standing under him own Tamarind, a stone take him forehead make bull's-eye. He bleed a steady red. Another stone miss him and sink inside the Tamarind bark. Some gum fluid trickling out of it. Anancy turn way from the pickney slingshot them and watching the gum fluid dripping from the tree. He touch it and saying: "You knifin' you own fait' in salvation. All you man an' 'oman, you sendin' up you pickney them for sacrifice. Them soul goin' get damn for good, an' the village goin' lost. Look how you pickney writin' out you fate 'pon the Tamarind. Them draw blood an' it goin' res' 'pon you 'ead, for ever an' ever."

After that piece of stoning, Anancy draw way himself, and good thing too, just as the police preparing to make a grab and arrest him. For a whole month, the people in the Area township don' hear a thing about him. Then, one night sudden, the village hearing one set of screaming and bangarangs coming from Heaven Corner. And when the village people gathering, what you think they seeing? The Tamarind chop down clean, and right 'mongst the tall cane shoot them and wild plantain, they hearing Anancy shouting out: "The word gone from all o' you. The life that I could give you deny you gone for all time. You been listenin' to the commandment o' sin an' obeyin' too often. I able to see darkness. You mus' believe me. I able to 'ear darkness rumblin' over you 'eads, an' wha' I got to tell you is this: the word gone!" He pause the shouting little bit. The crowd full motionless. Then he saying: "The word can return 'mongst you. It can return, if you let it." He pause again. Then backing back, he saying: "You understan' wha' I been sayin'? I know say that the word can come back, if you want it to come back."

One or two people who been listening Anancy that night say that they see a certain woman dragging way the dead limbs of the Tamarind nearish towards Heaven Corner. They insisting blind that the woman bound to be a dead stranger. One by-

73

standing man that night describing what he see, something like so : " Well, I jus' listenin' usual to 'ow Brer Anancy carryin' on, an' all o' a sudden, me eye catch sight o' a 'oman in a flowin' sort o' robe, sort o' t'in gauze business, runnin' way an' draggin' some tree limbs after her. She runnin' up to Heaven Corner top. Well, as I seein' this t'ing, I decidin' to see if anybody else seein' too. I turn to Anna, who is me own gal pickney, that same one, an' I sort o' nudge her in her side, an' the chil', Anna, did well see exac'ly wha' I did see, you know. That right, 'cause she been lookin' like she want to faint way wit' frighten on me right dere an' den. I frighten bad, too, I tellin' you that now. An' Anna never utter a word, as the Bible say. Some other people them did see, an' they stan' dere an' never utter a word. We all did see it but we never make a' utterance, as the Bible say. Boun' to be duppy. Tha's wha' I truly t'ought at the time an' tha's wha' I t'inkin' right now, talkin' to you. Tha's all I can say."

After that night fright episode, the villagers them don' hear gun fire no more about Anancy. But as Sister Granma Ethel continuing her story of what happen to her, I start feeling that Anancy hut carrying more spider mysteries attach to it than spider web. A funny feeling reach me that say that the hut can tell me more than I learn from the old lady herself. Sister Granma Ethel telling me that Anancy return to him wattle-and-daub and retire there. In the village, the Spidering Church reclaim-up it stray-way worshippers and as there be no other Anancy distraction or botheration, everything pass over smooth as nase-berry. Sister Granma Ethel say that one day, while she searching for few piece of bramble for firewood, she spy Anancy. He grow a proper horror black beard and age considerable like. She say that she say to herself on spot : " Coo-ya! I's ghos' or wha' stan' up in front o' me? " She say he look as though he in crying need of a woman hand. He look old bad and mad. She follow him up to the hut. Then she saw things that still haunting her. And that so why Sister Granma Ethel start begging me to drop the search. She say that things she see up there too terrible. She saying all this but even then I really didn't catch on too good. She end up her story abrupt-like, like this : " You see, Brer Oversea, I been t'inkin' that Anancy really did love to talk the 'Oly Word. Him really did. Come wha' can come, that was

74

him spidermos' callin'. Him jus' had to preach. You can say he anoint that way to such a' exten' that he jus' simple had too much of a bad love for preachin' the 'Oly Word."

So, I decide to drop the investigation business 'mongst the villagers them. I decide to give the Area township a walk. I wanting to prove Sister Granma Ethel story. So, the Monday night of the third week of me stay in the Area, I leaving again for Heaven Corner. I wearing a pair of sampatas and creeping cat up the hill that leading into Anancy reserve. As I passing the Tamarind stump, some wicked mosquito them slashing me foot and face, left, right and centre razor blade, and humming a hive, something like dive bomber, round me shoulders and ears. I dodging them brisk and circling the last cane field and edge-edging towards the clearing. I reach in the reserve. I belly crawl-ing and getting nearish a clump of macca bush. Then I stopping and peeping over the heap of prickles standing up like guard. Anancy not too far off in a wide corner in the clearing with him head fling back like cigar box lid. The beard pointing finger to the sky in a weather vane shape. The eyes like cut glass, and as he turning, side to side, they flashing neon. He speaking in tongues and using a muffle-up voice. Then he coming out of the tongues and speaking plain. Hear him : " You! You, up there so! Wha'ever you name, I come again to say you words. I come to spread you words roun' the four corners o' the worl' to all who won' listen." He pause and jiggle him neck.

I watching him close. He jiggling him body, one, two, three time, shimmy. I thinking that it must be a definite holy exercise him doing. It look funny.

Then he continuing : " All them who 'earin', listen good, an' them who wishin' not to 'ear me, make them visit the hall below the hill an' enter into the shame o' the service belongin' to the Spiderin' Church." He pause the flow and mopping him fore-head with a dirty rag. Then he fling it on the ground and take three stride over to where I standing, and stop sudden soldier. I thinking he see me but he looking up to the stars and the black-ness between. The muffle-up voice beginning again. The talking in tongues going on fast no propeller.

I watching Anancy toes. They scratching dog into the ground.

75

The toenails like short bramble stick, curve round the tips and clawing the dirt. They discolour bad. He going on digging them deep into the ground as he mumbling in tongues. The discolouration getting worser. Then I hearing him surfacing from the tongues with this plain talking: " I 'ave plenty name: Samson, Job, Moses. I 'ave peace o' min', an' wit' it I goin' serve you cause down 'ere 'pon the lan' to the end o' me preachin' days."

As that finish, he dig him chin into him chest and shriek a spike animal sound. And then it happen. Sister Granma Ethel story dragging itself right out in front of me own two eye. The hut door swing clean open and a spider boy come out dress-up to forty-nine in embroider Spidering Church vestments. He holding two big blue candle 'gainst him chest. He putting them down on the dirt yard and going back into the hut. Anancy looking up, then sinking him chin into him chest dog-fashion and screaming again. It even more whistle perfect then the first time. The spider boy coming out again and he carrying two green candle, cradling them on him chest. Then come one more round of the same said carry-on and the boy putting two big pink candle beside the blue and green one them on the dirt yard.

Meantime, Anancy been like a cage animal, moving short and long, up and down. He beginning uttering a low howl with some kicking and 'nough snorting. He swinging him arms and legs like clock hand and circling the reserve frantic. After some seconds, the boy child bringing out a whole tray of skulls and bones. Most of them come from dead brother, sister, dogs and cats. He putting them in rows in front of Anancy who standing cool priest with him head slanting far back. Then Anancy working now. He propping up the skulls and bones with aurelia bush. The Bible them of three colours set out like ceremony on one of the three stool I did notice on me first visit. The boy child bringing out two more stool and ranging them in a wide V before the skulls and bones. The bottle them with the mahogany lean-to come out last of all.

Anancy wearing cucumber quietness. He numb still and glaring at one of the skulls, like say it a relative or somebody. He staying in this numb position 'til the boy child come before him. Then he raising him right arm, whistling simple and turn-

76

ing to the hut door. The boy child leaving from beside Anancy and walking into the hut. Then he coming back with a box of matches. Anancy looking satisfy. He smiling a leader smile and fingering a beckoning to the boy child. As he walking 'cross to Anancy, the boy child smiling, too, and before you could say "Busta Backbone", a real animal scream happen, and the aurelia bush beside me to the left start one piece of shaking, shey-shey dance. The scream coming from the hut. I hearing it again. It sounding like the screaming of a woman animal. A next animal scream come. This time the boy child spinning six, seven circle and landing on him stomach. The he crawling on him knees 'til he reach the cradle them. Plenty sweat beading him face and dripping way splashes down him chest and thighs. Anancy sweating a stream too. The boy child drawing nearish the grinning skulls. He facing them now. Just then, Anancy shouting a soldier order militant in tongues, but the boy child understanding it. He hanging him head 'cross the back of the chair. Anancy walk over to him and finger pat him. He swing round and face the hut. He smiling cute. The boy child pick up the box of matches and hand it to Anancy. He choosing three sticks from it and throwing the rest over him shoulder on the left. He handing the three matches to the boy child and stepping back. A scratching sound come and a light showing on the boy child face. He passing him fingers over the candle wick them, touching the flame soft ceremony. He moving tiptoe. The light-up candle them flinging 'nough reflection on the hut side and on the skull faces. Anancy and the boy child bowing nice to each other. Anancy bowing lower than the boy child, and when he coming up back, he bounce him head on the child chest. He placing him hands on the child nose and bowing German from the neck. All this seeming to me to be some sort of private manners or something, 'cause the boy child not answering back with the same said gesturing at all. Anyway, the candle them flickering in the bad hush in the night. Anancy and the boy child standing double statue. I wondering what going happen next time go round. The mosquito them humming bees in me head. The waiting seeming too long. Sudden, Anancy clicking him fingers. The two of them bowing to each other and moving way from the hut entrance. The door banging open. The wattle-and-daub raining showers down the sides of the upright them. Anancy and the boy child peeping direct into the hut blackness and waiting Job. Another wattle shower raining down. Then a' animal scream. And a woman, with a heap of blood streaming down her face like birthmark, coming out of the hut blackness. She run out to the yard. She wearing a gauze thing clinging nightgown to the blood soak parts 'gainst her thighs and ankles. She passing the skulls, like she inspecting them for grinning on parade, and then she sitting on the third stool. Anancy staring blank at her and moving on winking at the boy child. Then, Anancy saying : " Correc' work, me son. Mos' good work." He start walking majesty over to the Bible them. He opening all three and standing watching the woman cat licking the blood from her lips. Anancy smiling, please as puss. The boy child idling relax, scuffing a pretty pattern shape with him foot in the dirt and answering back Anancy smile. Little after, the boy child looking sheepish sort of, ducking him head and waiting for something to happen big.

Then a deep animal moaning starting up, and the woman collapse like a matches house. As she drop, Anancy brace himself, rub him hands over the blue Bible and beginning the Mass : " The lesson I take from a tex' o' Sain' Paul Gospel : ' For I was alive wit'out the Law, once; but when the commandmen' came, sin revive an' I died.' "

Just right then, just as if they answering back telephone call, the skull them looking like wind-rain bleach guards and seeming to rock, back and front, grinning so-so-mockery.

ANANCY AND THE QUEEN HEAD

ANANCY AND THE QUEEN HEAD

Story starting on anniversary day celebration when every man Jack 'membering the 'mancipation of the spider slaves them. The day gone long time from the actual freeing day, if you see what I meaning to say to you. So, now, 1st of August, the day, a Sunday day time. Brother Sun bright everywhere with a raw vengeance. Right on top the cassias them that standing guard over the Park playground plenty humming-bird pecking blossoms wild as fart, and dropping and swaying shey-shey in a puff blowing through Spanish Town. The Square nervous facing expectance, and things. In Brother Sun ace light, big-time Rodney Memorial wash and polish recent, winking a 'quint, on and off, lighthouse, as few stray beam them catching 'nough of the marble whiteness. The fence round Rodney hanging with cut roses. Down by the sidewalk, Brother Sun drying up the drop petals them and the scallops red and rubber like conch fringe. Round the Square, three, four spider man, woman and pickney dress-up bright in red, yellow and navy things, strutting turkey and giving Law for peas soup. Two spider pickney them dress like sailor and playing ass behind them parents. You should see them gazing question up at Rodney; you would dead with laugh to rass.

Not all that so farish off from the pickney, sitting three tight bundle, two old cobbler and a young spider man everybody calling Anancy. The two cobbler them fighting off the sun-hot in them usual ol'-time fashion, calling up dead-bury memories, mouth and lip, and thing.

Brother Joshua, the most ol' cobbler, bending down and caving in him belly and starting to put deep question to him companion, Brother Manuel. This one of them : " Look 'ere, now, Manny, you 'member Rodney Memorial some year ago? "

Brother Joshua and Brother Manuel the last rockstone ol' soldier them in Spanish Town. Anancy, feeling proper ignore and leave out, just sitting quiet with him tail lap and listening 'nough ears to the two ol' man them. He hear when Brother

Joshua putting the question about the Rodney statue, and he anxious to know how much Brother Manuel come-back going be.

Brother Manuel eyecorner winking and he spitting phlegm 'pon the dry dutty and beginning: " Yes, Josh, them was the days that Spanish Town was f'certain Spanish Town. No joke 'bout that at all, at all."

Right there so, Anancy thinking: " Even me 'ear 'bout 1st o' Augus' celebration in the ol' capital. So wha' the rass so special 'bout 'memberin' when freedom grant? Man free, an' that done an' gone. Wha''special 'bout it? " But like how he release the little piece of history, Anancy knowing say that he trying to keep up with Brother Joshua and Brother Manuel, and it causing him to feel knife twist deep inside. The pride thing getting knock bad. And Anancy resenting it like bitch. It making him feel him spider years soft no jelly, wobbling close next to the ol' man them hardness. So he reaching f'him cigarette box gangster style.

Brother Joshua and Brother Manuel looking round the corner of them eye like wizard and most dry. They catch the newness of Anancy Ronson lighter, as he putting it up back. Brother Manuel asking him for a light in him usual whisper voice. After this contac', Anancy not feeling as ol'-time ignore as he feeling some minutes gone, and it look like him small-time resentment don' got no edge like knife no more. He looking up at the Rodney thing and off again just as quick like, because he hearing Brother Joshua, betwixt the sucking noise on him clay pipe, beginning one piece of harking back deep down from a ring ol'-time dream that saying that: " So, then, now, this bad mis' o' suppression liftin' off the lan', yes! It liftin' off the lan' by coffee 'edge an' Manor outroom. Even Sister Auntie Becky grass yard an' the famous Market Place did hexperience it. As a matter o' fac', 'Awbolition Ack' was a the subjec', bright all 'bout the place. It like them Sunday suit that come out sharp after them weeks an' weeks o' them Sunday rain."

Anancy listening. He knowing for a fact that the mist lift itself long time ages back; it almost like ancient history, 'til the ol' cobbler them decide to drag it up fresh. Anancy small-time resentment coming back like penny rain. He saying to himself: " The ol' people them. Not'in' but Wilberforce an' Clarkson lef'-over! " Yet, all the same, Anancy knowing that the Square holding 'nough nervous foot, slow *mento,* ignorant bad about the tune or blind to the beat. And Anancy, seeing sudden plenty foot moving in chains, just simple bite him tongue and swallow him spit. Then he laugh a bad laugh. He look up at the cassias and dream that the blossoms meaning to tell him that he too young again. He gangster stub out him cigarette. He in a real dream. This time so, he wake up soft and want to keep up with the ol' man chatter boxing. Brother Manuel talking, and usual, the first few word always wash up betwixt cough-up phelgm and sucking-up noise on him clay pipe. Anancy manage to catch : " You know somet'in', Josh. Jerk you mem'ries far aback an' compare them days wit' these we 'mongst. No different disposition take we, nuh? Look 'ow them young boy an' gal spider pickney in these modern days jumpin' wit' joy as if joy is common item like some rockstone in river bottom. 'Member 'ow that Augus' 1st we 'cestors mus' be jump wit' joy when joy was real joy? Josh, times change colour bad. Yes, it change, from luscious redfruit to a dutty, dutty brown."

Brother Joshua bowing him head in ol'-time yes. He making a one knock, two knock on him Adam apple and saying : " Yes, Manny, the day o' the real Spanish Town gone too far from we, nuh. But total everybody singin' still, yes. True. Them still singin' freedom 'pon top o' them small voice." In the nearish distance some strain of a spider political campaigning song rising and falling, poopalick, in a sort of usual church-time minor key. After two bar pass, Brother Manuel adding this to him speech : " But listen to wha' them young people singin'. I tellin' you, now, that that sort o' singin' boun' to be a sad business. This modern song sad an' sour out o' this worl' f'true nuh."

That crack a big hole in Anancy. The resentment boiling up to spitting. He refuse admittance that f'him days could sad so. He got to balance off the feeling. He thinking of him spider woman at home, sweet pussy and thing. He sure of him rice and peas dinner and him outsize egg custard, and him half pint of Black Seal rum. On a Saturday night time, the Town Hall dance or a brokings round the corner to go to. Sunday come, he could depend on Brother Tacuma week ol' domino tournament. And during the week, too, the theatre down the road showing either

83

a gangster picture or the latest cowboy film. 'Course, these ancient cobbler them in bad dotage and not too casere in them head either. So Anancy thinking. And he not even sure that them can still mend shoes, when it come to that. He feel like shouting them down. He want tell them that : " You days done. You ol' bumpkin, you, you function stop braps. You ol' an' sof' in you ways, that is wha'. You can't see that the times callin' f'new 'andlin's, new ideas an' new spider man wit' a whole 'eap o' courage an' 'igh studies. Everybody attitude mus' change, mus' look up an' drif' way from the blasted 'Awbolition Ack' simple 'cause the times callin' f'that sort o' fashion. Every move an' man an' t'ing boun' to College up an' technical an' science can't done. We mus' wake up an' advance to modern 'quirement o' fire politics an' f'we ownership. You can't see wha' goin' on all roun' you? The ol'-time days change. Ask anybody if they not free an' chain-up different. Ask anybody."

He turn off the venom. He know that they would perhaps, perhaps not, hear him and then dismiss him as a modern ' moonshine baby, moonshine mad '.

He hear when Brother Joshua saying : " Yes, I tellin' you, Manny, the song them singin' sad."

And he hear when Brother Manuel answering : " All the same though, some tune mellow wit' the years like rum in a cask."

To this pretty piece of deepness, Brother Joshua more than usual excited, and he answering back strong and crips. Hear him : " True word, Manny. But hol' on there : mellow sometimes another way o' sayin' spoil. 'Member, Farmer Boy cow 'ave calf in a 'aste an' calf get fat while cow drop down dead 'pon bank side."

The ol' cobbler them bu's a laugh. Then they spit some ugly phlegm few foot off into the dry dutty. And the dutty close finger round the two pool making them favour two half-close eye cover down under heavy eyelid.

Anancy raise himself up slow and stand straight. As he strolling off, he hear when Brother Manuel saying : " True word. Mos' true word, Josh. True like Atom over yonderlan'."

Anancy crossing the Park playground and taking the east gate for the street. He jerking him belt cowboy cocksure and he deciding to give Brother Tacuma a look-in to see how things

84

going at the domino tournament.

As Anancy walking on he silent mute as stone thinking about the exchange betwixt the ol' cobbler them. He feeling there must be some sort of dawning morning somewhere lay down waiting to get pick up. Like some sort of Anancy born again, if you want put it so. A real spider special thing that going carry with it a beat like shey-shey.

He nearish Brother Tacuma house and inside spitting space of the campaign meeting going on high session. He considering the singing he hear early back. It in full flow now. Microphone, loudspeaker, banner, pan-head police in attendance and a spider crowd heckling and shoving like ants. Anancy nearish 'nough and listening. He watching the big-time speaker who a sort of stentorian man. He stoutish and sweating rivers. As he wipe him brow in one, him eye blood shot up travelling round and slipping down to rest on the most recent arrival, Anancy, young boy. Anancy shift on one foot to the other foot almost without breathing about it.

The speaker booming : " An' when I say that you is people o' Spanish Town, Sain' Cat'rine, I sayin' that you is people o' the worl' ! "

Anancy thinking to himself serious that that statement sound all right. It big. It proper.

The speaker man again : " So, people o' Sain' Cat'rine, we findin' a road, a journey to take, hard an' long, but a'ready, the dawn dawnin' f'we. Not a Moses dawn wit' doubt gather up back o' it either."

Anancy move along and edging towards Brother Tacuma fence. He hearing 'nough of what the speaker saying. He convincing himself that he spend too much time listening to other people farting round with word and such like. As he push the gate, he begin fumbling in him pocket f'a shilling which would most ensure him getting a playing seat round the leading domino table, No. 1. Sudden, bangarangs down the road. Anancy glance over him shoulder. He see the two ol' cobbler jostling them way through the crowd. Brother Manuel biting him clay pipe, while Brother Joshua brushing off the crowd like gingy-fly. Then Anancy see when Brother Blacksmith lick Brother Joshua a bitch

85

fist 'cross him face. Brother Joshua jerk two time, twitch and so, and fall down. He see the crowd move down on him. He hear Brother Manuel cry out a' ol'-time cry f'help. He hear Brother Joshua scream wildness. He hear a second scream. Then a long moaning. Then not a thing.

Anancy saying : " I better take out me shillin'; 'ead an' I give the cobbler them a 'and wit' the struggle; tail an' I mind me own business." He flip the shilling and it show the Queen head, plain as day. Anancy shove it into him pocket and head for the vacant seat at table No. 1.

The two cobbler can't never know that head did show no how. That is Anancy thinking on the subject, then and now.

ANANCY, THE ATOMIC HORSE

ANANCY, THE ATOMIC HORSE

The envious attacks of bad feeling 'gainst a good 'nough man name Brother Man forcing the said Brother Man to take foot and run into the forest lan's of the far country parts where he living with him wife, Sister Woman and them seven pickney. The envious attacks of bad feeling coming from all Brother Man friend contacts: him business dealers, political paseros and even him admirer them. Well, now, Brother Man safe and far from them malice brains aforethought.

The far country parts back o' beyon' bad. It a most out of the way place of total aloneness. It such a long alone place from anywhere else sort of place that Sister Woman had was to leave from early o'clock ages before sun-up time to go to Commercial Market and get the benefit like the worm and bird thing. And she don' get back 'til dusk come or nearish that part of evening time. Now, which ever time Sister Woman leaving her husband and them seven pickney, Anancy, in the shape of a massive mushroom head Atomic Horse, flying down and inspecting the Man and Woman family compound. The Atomic Horse having hungry eye f'the seven pickney. 'Course, Brother Man knowing how ring dangerous the Atomic Horse is. He seen some of the devil miseries it bringing to people a'ready, and he having some terrible doubt about the looks of the Atomic Horse in the forest lan's. He telling him wife about the Horse and giving her plenty husband warnings. So, one day, Brother Man saying to her: " You got to fix up the house early today mornin', 'cause I got to go out jus' after you gone. You goin' Commercial Market an' I goin' to the office of the Natural Assistance to Trappers Organization. I want order some foot trap f'capture the livin' daylights out o' the blasted Atomic Horse."

And Sister Woman saying: " But wha' 'bout the pickney them? Where they goin' stay? "

Brother Man: " They goin' be a'right today. The Atomic beas' don' show f'a whole week now, which mean he wanderin' far off."

89

So the house get fix betwixt them and Sister Woman feed the pickney and lef' them on them own alone in the compound. No sooner than clock hand gone about them business then the Atomic Horse walk inside the compound. The bitch beast scratch him mushroom head like travelling salesman thinking about involving up him customer in a heap of buying and *mucho* credit, and he saying: " Well, me lickle boy pickney, an' where you parents, eh? "

The boy pickney staring at the mushroom head and giggling behind him hand. He thinking it out of this world and look like 'nough clouds fattening on top of one another.

The Atomic Horse repeating him question, and the boy saying: " Them gone out, sir."

" Where you mother? "

" She gone Commercial Market in town."

" An' you father? "

" Gone f'buy some foot trap down the office o' the Natural Assistance to Trappers Organization, sir,"

" An' wha' you father goin' go do wit' him foot trap them, lickle boy? "

" I not too sure, sir, but I t'ink he mus' be t'inkin' o' mashin' up the Atomic Horse."

" He t'inkin' o' doin' that, lickle boy? "

" Yes, sir."

" He t'inkin' o' mashin' up the Horse life jus' so, lickle boy? "

" Tha's wha' I t'inkin' he t'inkin', sir."

" I see."

The Atomic Horse putting two and two together and not getting twenty-two at all no how, and then he turning him mushroom head like say it doing some sort of radar work up in the sky, and when he doing that thing, the boy pickney down below hearing a click, then another click, one after another, 'til ten click come and gone. The clicking counting themself back from ten, like so: nine, eight, seven, six, five, four, three . . .

When it reach nought, the Atomic Horse give himself a steady piece of shuddering and swoop no eagle and swallow up the boy whole one time like soda dumpling in a red peas soup. It a most quick operation and all lef' was a sort of double crater hole, two bare foot mark where the boy been standing up and talking the time of day with the Atomic something.

So, now, every time the poor unfortunate Brother Man had was to go way to look about him foot trap, and Sister Woman had was to go Commercial Market, the Atomic Horse come into the compound and gulp down one more of the Man-Woman pickney. But so it happen now that day seven come and the table turn f'everybody concern with the bad business, 'cause when the Atomic Horse was just going swallow down the last of the seven pickney, Brother Man return back to the compound in the nick. He walk slow up behind the Atomic Horse who talking sweet cloud to the pickney number seven. The Horse saying : " An' tell me, now, lickle boy, where you father? "

" He gone f'buy some foot trap down the office o' the Natural Assistance to Trappers Organization, sir."

" An' wha' you father goin' go do wit' him foot trap them, lickle boy? "

" Mash you one time ! "

And just as the Atomic Horse going giant gulp down the boy, Brother Man take out one of him brand new shining foot trap, circle it cowboy over him head, aim it high sky and make it fly right over the fat body of the Horse slups ! A real splish-splash noise, a soft explosion, and the Atomic Horse get destroy, but not before he manage to gulp down Brother Man last pickney, number seven.

Quick 'mergency, Brother Man run into a thick clump of bush-john, pick a handful of berries and come back to the dead body of the Atomic Horse. He rip open the belly of the Horse, take out him seven sons them and squeeze the juice of the bush-john slap into the dead eyes, fourteen of them, straight down the line. One by one, they coming back to life in the compound, restoring up to them natural body self and looking like boy pickney and how they born to look. Brother Man most proud in him feelings as he watching the reborning going on in front of him living eyes same place. He calling him wife now, him voice showing ownership plenty. The voice catch her just as she coming inside the compound with a heap of groceries from Commercial Market.

Brother Man saying : " Sister Woman, come an' see 'ow I get back we seven boy pickney them from the Atomic Horse."

91

Sister Woman come up and she crying mixtures. Her face showing sadness and gladness, turning on and off, like peeny-walley dark night time.

The nine of the Man-Woman family standing nine columns in front of the compound house, like say unity bound to be strength in days of strain and such bothers. This the picture 'til the seven boy pickney them forming a sort of half moon formation and beginning asking them parents these certain questions: First Son: "Why you bring we back when you know that there always goin' be a' Atomic Horse?"

Second Son: "You couldn' see that we dead an' 'appy?"

Third Son: "You mean to say that you believin' that the Natural Assistance to Trappers Organization really got a new plan in store f'we, after 'ow them let you down so often?"

Fourth Son: "Wha' sort o' fool-fool people you at all, f'trustin' Organization when Organization can't even mash them tea bread?"

Fifth Son: "Why you didn' min' you own business an' let we res' in peace?"

Sixth Son: "Wha' we life goin' go be now? F'you own or f'we own?"

Seventh Son: "You can't see we did give way everyt'in' name Hope? Don' you know wha' that mean?"

Brother Man and Sister Woman couldn't answer one of the questions, don' care how they trying hard deep down inside themself, straining like madness and hoping to come up with something ol'-time and wise. So, the seven boy pickney them close in on Brother Man and Sister Woman, form a ring, dance round little bit, stop, shuffle foot, gather speed, stampede and kill them on the spot baps.

As Brother Man and Sister Women kicking them last in the dirt, Anancy, shaping up as another Atomic Horse, screwing him neck round the corner of the compound and laughing mushrooms can't done.

THE MAN NAME PEACEFULNESS

THE MAN NAME PEACEFULNESS

'Cause of him massive Monument calmness and sharpness no dove, and 'cause him handsome as handsome do, a certain young spider man call Anancy calling himself Peacefulness. As a most plain naturalness of this face card fact, a whole heap of hard breathing woman them having blood desire to come as him wife for life. But Peacefulness saying no to all them advances and wishes in the marriage matter. Peacefulness not playing hard to get; he just simple born hard to get. Family trait.

So, now, the brokings come to the village. The dance brokings is a bitch thing. Three young gal coming to the brokings, and Peacefulness seeing them and liking them, not separate, but as a group of fruit, fresh and juicy. He taking quick romance into him head and walk slow and saying to himself and to few others standing nearish: " If only one man could marry off t'ree gal one time, I would do that small matter right now f'meself. In fac', them t'ree gal is the firs' set o' flesh I seen that I want as me own."

But everybody telling Peacefulness that life don' go so at all, that he mad bad having such brain and body feelings. Everybody climbing up and begging the Monument not to get catch by the three piece of sweet pussy. Everybody bowing low dirt and begging bags of begging that he don' say yes to the moonshine feelings. But Peacefulness just looking on and sighing romance and thing after the gal them.

Well, now, to rass! When the people decide that they can't bear it no longer, they draw round in a wide out circle round Peacefulness and dead up themself with shut mouth and glass eye. It work good.

Peacefulness get bothers and asking them: " An' wha' the meanin' o' all this circle o' silence formation roun' me for? "

Brother Speechman, the main mouth of the circle, stepping forward and saying: " Mos' democracy goin' sour lately, an' so we can't hol' we tongue. F'a long time, now, you been f'we own Peacefulness, meanin' peace o' min' an' all that. You been wit' we an' we lovin' you wit' all we 'eart an' taxes. We don' want to see you destroy youself in a young gal spin head sickness. This a matter we can settle quick f'you, right here so. We can sen' the t'ree gal back where them come from."

And Peacefulness say : " Destroy meself? "

" You goin' mash up youself, if you follow after them t'ree sof' trap, sure as pussy got teet', front an' back."

" But that boun' to be foolishness, man. F'me name is Peacefulness, an' total every action I take got to be all correc' an' lucky."

" Not wit' pussy."

" Wha' make so then? "

" Well, Peace, the position stay so, 'cause them t'ree gal pickney you wife-desirin' not t'ree gal at all, at all."

" Wha' them is, if them not t'ree gal, Brother Speechman? "

" I tell you. I want you believe me when I tell you that them t'ree gal not t'ree gal in the flesh no time at all. Tha's all I want you know f'the time bein', Peace."

" I not takin' that jus' so, Speech. You got to convince me. Wha' them name? "

Brother Speechman think little bit. He feeling the burden heavy no ton weight. He square off. He swallow hard. Then he coming up with this : " The firs' gal name Russ. The secon' gal callin' herself Ame. An' the t'ird one got the greetin' card o' Gra B."

" Mos' funny names, Brother? "

" Mos' funny gal them, Peace."

" Meanin' wha, Brother? "

" Meanin' that them not really gal. Them is rockets! "

But Peacefulness not going in that direction at all. He not going get side track from him romance and thing. He belly laugh, and Brother Speechman feeling lost and found and lost again in the sound of Peacefulness mocking him.

" Speech," Peacefulness saying, " I don' care if them is rockets or launchin' pad or boosters or any other piece o' ironmongery; I goin' married all o' them, one, two, t'ree! The t'ree goin' be me life long wife an' we goin' live 'appy together 'til kingdom come."

Now, Peacefulness got a mother and a father standing nearish him when he saying the mouth full. They hearing him words and deciding that Peacefulness not the sort of son to back down, even f'a mother and father sake. So is policy now. With plenty jinnalship, they considering to run them mouth 'gainst the three gal and rub out the prospects that just get announce to them by Peacefulness. So, the mother saying: " Me son, Anancy, who is Peacefulness own self, very much in a sof' condition over you t'ree sweet gal pickney. I, as him firs' woman, so to talk, goin' sugges' you all come make decision which one o' you the mos' pretties' o' the t'ree. The one who win the contes' goin' get the lovin' o' Peacefulness. Wha' 'bout it then? "

They hearing the jinnalship but they not recognising it at all. They gather up together and confab breaking 'mongst them.

Russ say: " Don' like. Don' trus'. Don' want."

Ame saunter little bit and say : " I jus' as good as the nex'. Besides, I the younges' an' the readies'."

Gra B. say: " It not fair. I believe in me 'cestors an' them ways o' workin' out t'ings. Not'ing like muddlin' t'rou. Yet an' all, since you other two stickin' out. I 'ave to stick out too. We all 'ave plenty to protec', you know."

Well, then, the father of Peacefulness, a' ol'-time battle warrior man who 'custom to him guerrilla thing and thing, deciding to help out by making a suggestion too. He square off him soldier-ing shoulders and say : " The bes' t'ing is competition in the mountain fashion. Bush tactics never 'urt the bes' man. As a matter o' fac,' 'ill-side warrin' is a power, magic, eternal blessin' 'pon Eart'. It causin' Heaven to come down to we like rain. So, I sugges' you t'ree gal take youself way from this spot an' go in a private corner o' the bush an' fight it out like revolution. The winner goin' 'ave me son, Peacefulness who is the one an' only Anancy. After all, the whole idea o' 'avin' me son is to fight as 'ard an' as vicious as you can f'him. If you put all you 'eart an' soul into it, you goin' win Peacefulness as a 'usban' to live wit' f'ever."

Brokings come and pass. The dance beat fade. The three gal find a corner, change themself into three rocket which was them shape all the time, and they ready themselves to fight f'the hand of Peacefulness. Them sleek-up silver metal limbs shining pure space death to one another cold.

97

Russ shoot straight up in the air sudden and sharp no razor. Ame following after, but look like slipping back to Earth base right down. Gra B. staying put down foot and planning and watching the other two cautious, according to 'cestors and how them used to do things in the ancient. But Russ alone up there. Ame coming and going back down. All the same though, this one-woman rocket play not to go on for too long. Ame trying again, slipping back to Earth, but trying again, and then shooting straight up in the air to meet up with Russ. Ame start trying to knock Russ in her rass. The fight going on now with vengeance. Russ and Ame fighting east and west all about the place like mad ants. Them magic twain just refusing to meet on the subject of Peacefulness. But, all this time so, nice as a ninepence, Gra B. sprawling cool cucumber neutral on the ground. Then baps, Russ and Ame connect. They banging each other without thinking, and they starting one power dive full speed. When Gra B. seeing all this, she easing herself out of the way where the crater going happen in seconds. But Gra B. not quick at all. Russ and Ame drop flush 'pon top of her, and the three rocket burning steady crater for days.

Nine days gone and Peacefulness with him mother and father. He shaking him head sad and saying to them : " Me cause it. F'me fault. I should married the t'ree o' them an' they wouldn' feel inferior 'mongst themself."

And so, Peacefulness knowing that he have to live without softness for a long time to come. Maybe f'ages.

The father of Peacefulness raising him arms and saying : " I did know that them not f'you, me son. I knowin' that an' I fix it. I not sorry."

But it in the nature of Peacefulness to brood. He visit the crater every year end and watch f'a sign of life to prove him father wrong. He still waiting.

PEACE MEAL ANANCY

PEACE MEAL ANANCY

One time, there was a killing drought of food on the lan'. What I trying to say is that one definite sort of bickle call Peace Meal decide to scarce itself and give everybody a bad t'rill way down in the belly bottom. I trying to say, too, that the food name is Anancy, the same ol'-time jinnal spider man, shaping up in another shape. Only two smallish amount of Peace Meal growing anywhere on the lan'. The funny thing about the amount is that it got legs to walk on and it have a way of getting on most cute and escapish. Nobody, no bickle expert, no farmer man, no animal dress up as human being, no force, no committee, no nothing know how to trap the smallish amount of Peace Meal on the run. Total everything and everybody had was to starve Indian starvation and suffer heaps of body wants and brain needs, while Peace Meal walking garden naked in front of all the big eye them watching him in two parts on the lan'.

But Brother Cat, call by name Ama, strike a Peace Meal trapping plan. Cat got a giant supply of honey stock' up somewhere safe, and Cat take it and pave the road where Peace Meal taking a walk. And that is how Ama did manage to trap Peace Meal.

Brother Dog, call by name Ge Ban, feeling a real envious stab cutting him pride, come and hear the news of Brother Cat trapping of Peace Meal, and decide direct to make a come-back trap to hold the balance of Peace Meal, part two, and to put himself in the position of brainy trapper, as Cat do first. Well, the second half of Peace Meal walking into Brother Dog trap and walking out of it again, easy as saying " Peace on the lan' ". Dog most ignorant and distemper up with defeat. As a sort of last pride resort, Dog deciding to jump on Peace Meal back and bringing it to ground, but Peace Meal not going get check so no how; instead, Peace Meal riding off like horse with Dog. And as that happening, Dog esteeming self collect a bitch blow and letting out a long piece of howling all over the lan'. Dog

101

shouting : " F'the sake o' Commonpoverty o' animals in the worl', please, Brother Cat, save me from this secon' piece o' Peace Meal. Ama, me frien', save me! "

Brother Cat hearing Dog; nothing not wrong with Cat hearing. But Cat wait little bit before he head into the saving business. Final, he move and save Dog and trap the balance of Peace Meal. So, both the first half of Peace Meal and the lately trap balance of it come together 'cause of the action of the two brothers, Ama and Ge Ban. They looking at them capture, and each brother starting to have a real greedy feeling washing him head bad. The unite amount of Peace Meal laying down before them making them having botheration and plenty studies in Q.

Cat saying : " F'me name is Ama an' I can't live 'pon f'me one piece o' Peace Meal alone. I need f'you balance to make me 'appy an' satisfy."

Dog saying : " F'me name is Ge Ben an' I want know why you needin' f'me balance o' Peace Meal. Why so? "

Cat drawing breath and saying : " 'Cause I can feed more people than you ever able f'feed. F'me lan's more 'portant, younger an' more 'gressive than f'you own. That make why."

Dog : " Tha's a lot o' rass you sayin' to me, Ama, an' you know it. Look the lan's I 'ave over yonder an' far away. I needin' f'you Peace Meal so me job do proper."

Well, now, they leaving them capture Peace Meal and beginning to shape up for a boxing match. The fight calling itself : DOG VS CAT PEACE MEAL EART' CHAMPIONSHIP FIGHT O' FIGHTS.

The battle silence before the actual fighting depressing and powerful. The trees quiet. And the stones. And the rivers. And one big belt tie round Nature belly, making her saying nothing at all.

Dog expert with 'nough fights behind him tail, when him was in him young days. Cat don' have much back history but Cat young and have beach muscles under him crew-cut body.

The lashing begin. Pure madness going on. Up and down. Crossways and sideways. Everything and everywhere. 'Til at last, the end come and Ama and Ge Ban kill themself with double twist back. And Peace Meal gather up itself, part one and part two, walking slow and considering the happening just

102

gone. Then it bend down over the dead spot, skate eye on the remnants, shake head two time and walk way whole and Anancy.

SEVENTEEN

SEVENTEEN

This particular Anancy coming to you as a spider man with seventeen mothers to him credit. Believe me, now : when I say that that is the mystery of things, I mean it like I never mean anything else before. But even though he got all them seventeen mothers, with bands of love round him, he having son respect f'total only one of them. He hating the other sixteen with a monster hate that terrible to witness just so. You must try and understand that the looks of son hatred is a baffling thing, outside Hell and flood water, to consider plain and straight. This Anancy so hating him large mother excess that he growing quiet and mad with a ring anti-mother sickness, lock up deep inside him, day in, day out. He getting no ease-up at all from the state of anti-mother mind, hard as he trying to dodge it. Everything with woman shape, S-design, soft meaning, pussy resemblance and belly 'sociation making him aerated bad in him head. If he see spoon or scissors or cup or sack or crookstick or a Y, poor Anancy get into a rawtid botheration.

Some days, he sit and wonder about the clutches the mothers force him to live inside, and direct, he start hatching some bitch plan to mash up the mother welfare state that licking him shirt and ringing him balls like ice cream bell Sunday four o'clock time. When he come out of the ruling class moody and get back into him rebel self with a don'-care physog, he jump up and web write, on the nearest tall wall, in him street, the following piece of caution : GO HOME SIXTEEN !

All the same, Anancy don' too relish them moments of self-closeness at all. They making him take notice of other powers and make him feel he draining way on the lan'. This sort of small eye cutting up him spider calmness and brutalizing him national spider pride. After a brute try, he trying to capture back him true spider cool. He catching a glimpse at the family picture of the seventeen mothers and figuring out what purpose the excess sixteen really serving him. He try and give the excess a cause for the powerful presence in him life, but not a thing reasonable dawn 'pon him no how.

You see: the bad drama about poor Anancy life was simple that he born a top hat spider in search of cloth and straw hat looking glass in living and bob and weaving. He imagine himself that big life got to touch small life at point. And the thing to do is find the spot and try repair the damage. And, you see: that sort of head move bad-worse than let-down, 'cause, after all, top hat and straw hat bound to make from total different material (or so Anancy secret believe true, 'special' when not a soul looking). So, now, the difference obvious bad.

Anyway, Anancy going on living same way in two conflict-up dead end f'time and half. He full up with tormentation and spite and doubt and catching plenty anxious worries. Everywhere he go, he get reminder. If he see statue in a 'nough public place, he look 'pon it, and sure thing it remind him direct about some wicked part of him top hat history. It remind him a whole heap of mashing up other people country parts, wholesale t'iefing and broke down life. If Anancy happening to pass a place with a' ol' history name attach to it, he seeing 'nough raw back and lash. He know that the makers of the history name did plough plenty money and tricks and gall and brains into the t'iefing business, and did send the gold back home safe and tie up with city string, and so he resenting the memory bothering him, as he passing by, catching big 'fraid about him split self, half and half.

One day time, when the memory riding him like rolling calf at night time, he check out on a long walk from the things and history names fencing him in, and he find himself alone in a field, stone dead can't done. He sit down and rest himself. But after a little shut eye, he discovering he nearing the tormentation again. He try stop himself, but it too late. He look round and see battlefield. He see top hat plans. The field not calm countryside no more, a rass. Mento gone. It just another history name. He get up and start going back to the set-up in town. He never look back one time. When he connect with the city, he feeling tight throat and muscle-up in him neck and chest. This always the case after a day out. But this time, Anancy thinking about him own mother welfare state, and he sudden knowing to himself that he got to do something quick and brisk about the over-flow in the house.

So, he ups and kill off the sixteen excess mothers and spare the life of the one mother he feeling a son-love for. And when he do that small thing, the remaining seventeent' mother looking total honour-up and dignify like. She even make a try and hold up her head and walk single out like a real proud thing on the lan'. And she send and call her only son, Anancy, the avenger. When he come to her, she reach out her fingers and touch him rock face like bread she touching for the first time early morning. Then she pull him down beside her and kiss him to show how she grateful.

All she doing is proving that she got a hundred mother power love lock way deep down inside her, if he ever want tap it and use it in him living. She give him one last mother kiss. And as she do that so, Anancy catch a creeping nausea running direct to him brains, where the history names lurking like t'ief, and he shame bad. So, he kill her, too.

GOLD, SILVER AND BRASS

GOLD, SILVER AND BRASS

Brother Anancy, one day, get tired of him own back yard. He say he tired of the false money happenings on the lan'. He say he up to him back teet' with fish head and small change. Life fuck-up bad. So, he decide to take a walk overseas.

Well, then, he go live in a lan' with 'nough strange brothers and sisters. Though they be spiders like himself, they looking different, and behaving themself cute, as if the difference must and bound to get known right there and now. They different with a bitch difference. You see: they different and most proud flesh. They most proud to make people find out that they different, and most proud to stay so and make everybody see and get puzzle. They striking Anancy as if they too different again to live. In fact, Anancy think the thing out long, and he say to himself that they behaving like they special gold, silver and brass things on the little piece of ground. That spin round the other way go so : the gold thing adding up to one sort of class; the silver thing to another class; and the brass thing to third and last class. Anancy discovering that these things actual come to ways of thinking out living, like when you come to think about youself and a next spider person. These three things like three fence without post and barb wire or any such boundary mark-ing at all. They seem as if they operating like a ghost fence separating one form from the next and last. The situation mash-ing up Anancy brains. But he C back in Q and try pluck him inside and pull out sympathies and thing for the ghost brothers and sisters, but nothing coming to come. So, he telegraphing understanding of the carry-on of the special gold, silver and brass people round him, and all of a sudden, one night, he get a line 'pon them, 'cause of the bad weather they born living under foreign f'ages. He reckoning that the lan' they 'habiting not invasion-proof. He get to hear say that the three division of living, ruling and dying really go so, 'cause the lan' not the sort of lan', from early o'clock, that could do without division.

To keep the spider living going, the people had was to chop up things and rule them as 'cording to that. Thinking all this division business, Anancy link the ages gone with the present days of gold, silver and brass, and he find that the linking fitting linen glove. So, Anancy understanding the GSB people from far. And that way, he managing to pick him ways and means through the sink holes in the set-up; and, same way, he almost learn to tip-toe 'mongst the things gold, silver and brass, right 'cross the lan'. He almost swallow the division medicine and even some of the anti-spider skin feelings 'gainst him personal. But that was one thing he wouldn't swallow one rass, plus the high-up treatment of gold on silver, the swcet-up from silver level to gold, and the low bearing of brass to gold and silver.

With the happenings going south in the new country parts, all Anancy could do is hope that the shit wouldn't catch him. But things going on. He hoping plenty hope but nothing not changing a blas'. So, he ups and leave overseas and check back to him own back yard. As he lan' in the place and about to kiss dutty, blessing it say he glad he get back to rock and all so, what you think he seeing standing up in front of him, right 'pon the home ground?˙He seeing a bitch-time sign carving up the lan' saying: SPACE F'ALL. ROOM F'SOME. NEW PROSPERITY CATCH WE. GOLD, SILVER AND BRASS.

SOOT, THE LAND OF BILLBOARDS

SOOT, THE LAND OF BILLBOARDS

You must be sort of gathering, by now, that Anancy got the travel thing in him blood, like say how mongoose got chicken on f'him mind most time. That bound to be the reason why Anancy take foot, one day, to another lan' where he arriving strange as sarsaparilla growing which part snow come from. In this particular lan' call Soot, Anancy find he able to read big billboard all over the place. He able do this easy, 'cause the lettering black and white and bright bad. The first one Anancy clap him eye 'pon go like so: RUN!

Nothing else add to it. Anancy think hard, as he standing facing the one word message; he waiting f'some small understanding to burs' 'pon him; he don' get none; so, then, he laugh cyah-cyah. He laugh particular at the bosify lettering. He thinking that the billboard don' really done paint proper yet. How man going know where f'run, if he don' catch no meaning other than just plain run? He feeling console-up and confuse, even though he able read it.

The second billboard Anancy see just like the first one; it go so: OURS. It favour the first one, black and white and bright, and nothing else write 'pon it but the one word f'we own. All the same though, Anancy seeing that the lettering got a purple touch that the first lettering don' have. This billboard puzzling Anancy little bit, but, as 'cording to him nature, he start forget the whole thing. One fact about Anancy: he the most forgetting spider man you could find anywhere at all. He develop that forgetting forgiving side of him life to such a total point that he count it as him one bank balance. He get that way from the early days when licks used to ride him back and lash it plenty.

Well, anyway, Anancy stay cool in the sun-hot that Brother Sun been spitting out long time in Soot. And he forget the two sign them, the lettering and the entire billboard, big as life as them be.

He take foot and go into a part of Soot call by name Somethingville. When he get there, he hear about a Spiderman who

117

happen just to receive a vicious neck-hanging. Anancy, with all him blind eye way of looking at the strange country, couldn't help seeing how everybody seeming content and righteous, like they just done do something to make them clean and white inside.

Well, now, f'some Gawd reason that don' have explanation f'itself no how, Anancy change him spider man appearance by catching a wash in a cask of white paint, so that he come out white, as if he born to it nice and natural foreign. Then, in him white condition, Anancy walk up to one of the 'abitants of Somethingville and ask, speaky spokey, about what happen. The 'abitant tall and cough a proud lynch cough and crinkle him mouth corner, plantation boss, and answer with a sugar nod and say : " Where you from? "

Anancy say : " I from foreign. Why you wan' know? "

" Well, you won' find too much interes' in 'angin' 'mongst we in these parts."

And Anancy ask : " 'Ow come? "

And the 'abitant say : " 'Cause we' jus' ordinary folks 'roun' 'ere so, law-'bidin', goin' on usual."

So, Anancy ask : " But you too cool, man. I mean to say : you can cool 'bout other t'ings that 'appen; you should 'dignant bad 'bout the proceedin' o' this brutalisin' business o' 'angin' a man. You don' t'ink so, nuh? "

" 'Dignant 'bout it? No, stranger man. We not 'dignant at all 'bout 'angin'."

" Wha' you know 'bout it? You personal, I mean? "

" Well, as a Somethingvillean, I know this one fac'. It don' do by none o' we livin' roun' 'ere, at no time."

" But 'ow come you know that? "

" 'Cause we don' got no motive, stranger. As the man say, ' A man don' eat unless he feel 'ungry an' him belly makin' noise.' "

" So, wha' 'appen then? "

" The mos' I can say is that we glad the kidnappers them didn' come from f'we parts roun' so. We t'ink they mus' be come from far, somewhere out o' town, an' tha's wha' I been tellin' the Feelin' Brains Institute o' spider questioner them wit' me own words, lickle before you come."

118

" An' wha' the Feelin' Brains Institute man them say? "

" Not a t'ing wort' mentionin'. It always 'ard f'tell wha' the Feelin' Brains Institute man them imaginin' in them special brains, you know. 'Ard no bitch ! "

" So, wha' the local 'abitants them 'ave to say? "

" All o' we was 'opin' an' prayin' f'somet'ing to come o' the investigatin', 'cause we did wan' catch a listen to the case in court. We no goin' get the chance f'do that now, seein' as wha' 'appen."

" Not a link is a link, then? "

" No local connection wit' the 'angin' at all."

" 'Ow come that no jailer wasn't 'pon spot when the Spider-man get drag way an' 'ang? "

" Well, you see, stranger : jailer usual go 'ome when night come. He live only few yards up the road an' he usual go 'ome evenin' time early. Not a t'ing 'ceptional 'bout that, see. It be a normal peaceful Friday night in a normal peaceful law-'bidin' town. Somethingville like that. So we stay. So we get on. From long time, now. Mind we own business. An' law-'bidin'."

The next day, when Anancy leaving Somethingville and Soot, and he passing the two billboard them, he catch a look at him body whirling whiteness in a fast car flashing 'gainst him in the road, and he realise say that he did forget him change skin-colour, as you would expec', seeing what a most forgetful spider he be from morning; and so, he look down 'pon the put-on whiteness and laugh cyah-cyah, and he decide that he got to rub it off before he get back home to him yard good and proper.

But the whiteness catching bad, 'special if you have long 'sociation with it and got little bit settle way deep down. You see : the thing is that the white business take set in Anancy, and it taking long as rass to disappear and out-out from him skin naturalness. Little most it didn' get rub off complete at all. Anyway, when Anancy done get it off, he feeling like protection gone. He empty in a most funny way, but he fling ol' iron in him back and face himself and say that he back to normal, where all the back yard billboard them got f'him own message write as big as bitch. Even though that not the strict truth, it good f'Anancy think so 'til he wake up real one day.

119

IN YESSING MOUNT

IN YESSING MOUNT

Anancy living easy, hand to mouth, without plenty brain pain, f'years, in a place call Yessing Mount. Sudden the spot coming to be a place that actual causing everybody botheration and dark night happening. Anancy getting to hear about certain ace things making him spider aware and cautious extreme. Things going on, and after a while, he get conscious and bitter bad. This had was to happen, if you catching the sign I trying to point to slantways.

So, now, early 'nough one morning, some real bad news reaching Anancy. The news got volts and it shock him, 'cause it about a spider friend who they find with a long knife jam in him back, stone dead 'pon a pavement in the middle of Yessing Mount. F'the first time, Anancy start thinking about the division carving up in the malice actions 'mongst the 'abitants of Yessing Mount. He sudden get force to thinking about them as half so and half so : spiders and beetles; those on f'him side, and those on the other side; those who look like how him stay, and those who don' got no resemblance; those like him murder friend, and those who do the murdering; spiders and beetles. Yet and all though, there be a small section of the beetle population of Yessing Mount who trying them beetle most to make the murder look like a sort of robbery with V. But Anancy well know say that it be a simple broad daylight race case of beetle hating spider, and definite no sort of robbery with V, at all.

'Course, the penny got two side : plenty beetles wearing genuine draw down sad face. That same said something making Anancy take heart and feel that life don' necessary divide in two 'cause of how it complicate and lapping over, sometimes. These beetle personalities showing shame. They just as worried as Anancy and him spider personalities living round Yessing Mount. But other beetles having nasty ideas and beliefs by the dozen and causing Anancy to rub out the complicate thing and the lapping over feelings. These peculiar beetles believe in bad banners and dutty slogans. Anancy thinking heavy about lesson that got history attach to it, but he think so hard that him eye cloud over and get dim with heaps of hope that looking like it could be a dying thing 'pon him. He getting little confidence, now, in the shining law, tired no rainbow but still up there forming band 'cross everybody.

While all this studying knocking Anancy brain and fulling up him spirit cup, Yessing Mount getting bad name all over lan' and beyon'. This worrying the arse off a lot of the different thinking members of the beetle compound inside Yessing Mount and outside. The beetle police, who cute most time, when races going on so savage, earning a proper blackish name in and out the Mount. They working hard like small teet' comb, but they not finding the beetle, one or more, who kill Anancy spider friend. Yellow muscle contraction all about the place. And as if that not 'nough, sudden, a certain nasty beetle, travelling under the name Brother Anglo, decide to call a meeting of all beetle beating personalities. The meeting hold itself big in a Square far way from Yessing Mount. Not only beetles attending. And not only one type of beetle personality either, when the count take : worry-conscience, renovate nasty, earnes' student, rigid conservin', lovin' heart, curious not-movin' or un-budgin', stray, foreign-lan', Deep Soot, compassion, and simple awkward beetles.

The other side there, too. As a matter of story, they obvious black and white. You just had was to look round and you able pick them out like currants : bad-tempered politics, full complexion, 'alfie, those by 'traction, off-white, Asian, African, Carib, States-side, cute t'inkin', rabid, skirt an' blouse, wait-an'-see, factory, artis', and simple awkward spiders.

Things in the Square thin like wire and stretching 'lectric. Even the ordinary waiting f'the meeting to begin got a sound all it own. It got a buzzing sound, raw as rass. Right 'pon top of this, the knife voice of Brother Anglo coming. Some earnes' student beetles swarm with scarves move up and heckling technicolour. But that don' bother Brother Anglo. He start up again : " Firs', we goin' 'ear from the president official o' the beetle league, Brother Kickall! " The booing mix salt and pepper, and the president official get drown.

Anancy shaking him head despondent and walking way from the Square. He know that Brother Anglo and everybody going

124

lie like horse trotting about him dead spider friend. The lie bound to come. It going come strong, and he don' really want to know about it at all. So, now, Anancy feeling that him spider friend dead f'nothing. He calculate Brother Anglo deep, and then he walk on and lef' the Square. As Anancy turning out of the top part of the street, he see a long chalk-writing on a' ol' drop bomb wall. The writing read: VOTE F' BROTHER ANGLO. And f'the first time, since Anancy growing up, he realise that freedom not ordinary at all, that it hanging up like a long-time Spanish machete. And then he had was to hide him face and catch a laugh.

SPIDER HELL HOLE

SPIDER HELL HOLE

Two special ways to put down things and such like f'Anancy:
one way got to call itself prose business, like direct word using;
the other way got to do with poem. Mix up the two ways and
you getting something nearish a prose poem linking. Well, now,
the direct word personality in Anancy coming to the front part
of him everyday life sudden, one day, and he not able to put
check 'pon it. The power driving so strong that it like earthquake under him. The most he could do was mix the dynamo
feeling with a touch up from him natural poem personality. He
know the mixture going work wonders, if he don' look out. So,
the new mixture causing him to get on restless and torment-up.
When he coming on as a prose poem personality, he automatic
shove him slimish existence into a Spider Hell Hole, if you see
what I meaning. He feeling a full reservoir sensation all the
time, a sensation tall and bottle-up with actions and plans not
proper form in him imagination. All this up 'gainst him like he
got colic, like invasion by duppy. And when he in this condition, Anancy don' like meeting up with him friends. He staying by himself and living silent in him spider cool in him Spider
Hell Hole. He think that the exile business really the best thing
out to consider. He find that it hard no concrete to satisfy him
writing urging even when the Spider Hell Hole not in operation.

This particular day we talking about is the time when Anancy
prose poem side deciding to tackle a big-time writing thing. He
decide he going write in him own sort of way a number of newspaper article, leader, editorial, stop press item and sports result.
He having a grand time doing all this in the silence he enjoying
in him Spider Hell Hole. He full up with imagination, like
stubborn Jack and he feeling pack-up with ideas and muchness.
He convince himself that he bound to be more than one spider
inside himself, two or three possible. He sparking big brains and
'nough born promise, and producing some real masterful
language. When he finish him individual change-up of the last
set of football result, he breath a long-out creative breathing,

and like lightning, he know that he not only a real writer creature creating, but he also a first class Gawd artis', if the truth come to facts.

'Cause of this new thing, he feeling him pride big and high. He finger through him 'change-ups', giving them eye and nod. He smile a wicked smile and think about all the critic people and what they going say. Then he get depress same time. And so, he tearing up paper left, right and centre. Well, now, with him 'change-ups' gone f'all time, he had was to find something else to write to satisfy him prose poem personality. After pause and bad inspiration, he latch on to a projec' of prettying up advertisement and shop sign. He decide he going put new vibration and image thing into them, if it kill them and him. So, he work dynamo without looking to see if him shadow back of him, catching up or not. He walk round and take down in him spider prose poetry note book all the advertisement and shop sign he can clap eye 'pon and which he think needing prettying up. After three days out collecting, as if he some word merchant, he find he full up five note book complete. He proud. Then he reach back home and settle down in him room to burs' hard labour 'pon the wording he selec' during the time. He working piston. And he feeling a hot trickle sliding down from head to spine, as he dip himself into the job. This particular trickle meaning the world to him. He bathe in it. It quiet. He expert sort out the most important items and put them in order of what he call simple 'change', not 'change-up'. Although Anancy couldn't well call these items advertisement or shop sign, he register them in him note book, 'cause he think they need writing over bad. He gaze at them long and creative, and final, he work magic and change them with him prose poem imagination. When he done finish the score, he empty. Then, after he catch a space and rest himself, he turn and work magic 'pon others in them order of change. He twist them out of shape, worry them, argue with himself, chop and final convert them nature baggadam!

But Anancy not satisfy at all. He tell him first spider genius brains that he going try out working on the classify ads of a leading Area paper. First, he baffle, but he don' celebrate that f'long. Nothing like problem last where Anancy concern. Big

130

'fraid and humble crus' drop to nought minus. The attempt he making pleasing him no end. He push on hard and change all. And then, f'luck, he try out a' item in the personal column, and he change it bip bam! Not a trap is a trap. Everything smooth as glass. When he done him prose poem exercise at week end, he sit back and reading them loud. And he get one surprise. He see one time *baps* that he the most signifying writer he know anywhere.

And believe me : this worry him a lot.

ANANCY, PEOPLE PAINTER

ANANCY, PEOPLE PAINTER

Ages ago, Anancy was a promising painter of people face. F'him special line was a strange social phenom of a thing. You see: he only paint the face pictures of giants. They was the people he got most interest in, and none other. This phenom making Anancy art and Anancy himself plenty news. He get write up and 'nough coffee and bitch liquor drink in him name, while the phenom get spread all over the country, in all the loud-mout' Sunday paper, daily, weekly, monthly, quarterly and annual them. So far, to him credit, he paint Giant Unicorn, Giant Springbok, Giant Eagle, Giant Bull Dog and Giant Double-head Eagle, sitting down f'him, grateful can't done. But, then, sudden, one day, a heavy knocking tearing into him studio door, and when Anancy open it he see a' unusual client standing in front of him.

Client say: " I would a like you paint f'me face, Anancy."

Anancy 'quint two time, like say some foreign body get into him eye, and say: " Wha' you name? "

Client say: " Me name Flea."

Anancy look shock bad. He lock up himself in a deep silence. The size of the caller bothering plenty of Anancy idea of how giant must stay. This no giant at all. Giant can't so small.

Client say: " Wha' wrong? "

Anancy say: " Me can't paint you. I only paint giant. Sorry."

" But, Anancy, me's a giant! "

" No, man. You not no giant. You jus' a' ordinary flea, from down so, as far as I seein'."

" You wrong bad, Anancy. You behin' the time, late. Me's one o' the new giant them, springin' up all 'bout the place, recent."

" Me don' understan' wha' you sayin'."

" Well, Anancy, you see: me's a self-make giant flea, an' as such, me entitle to get paint by you. So it go these days."

' No, you not entitle to that at all. I never paint self-make nobody, in any shape or form, or f'that matter, no new giant,

135

self-make or not. I only paint those giant them who in register, giant who ol' not new, giant who arrive ol' by 'cestry an' 'istory, not 'tempo'ry self-make ones. I sorry."

Client say : " Don' sorry, Anancy."

But Anancy close the door and go back to him big studio. He sit behind him monster desk and contemplate the article of faith together with the boldness of the rising new. He also contemplate the letters to the Editor, news flash them and the rest that going report him refusing to paint the new giant flea, that is, if the NGF decide to take into him head to get him own back by reporting the refusing. It could ruin him chance of coming like a' international face artis'. Just as hc contemplating nightmare, he hear another knock tearing the studio door. He go out, open the door, and the same said flea standing up. Anancy bat him eye two time. The flea without motion, calm and compose. The way he standing looking like ace control. He seem to have plenty tight energy tie-up inside himself.

He say : ' I come again f'see if you changin' you mind 'bout me 'posal. I can pay anyt'ing you ask."

" Ownin' bank now ? "

" No, man. Jus' askin' 'ow much you goin' charge me."

" 'Ow much you t'ink I get f'me gallon size face pictures, Flea ? "

" Me don' know, Anancy. But wha'ever you top fee, Monday mornin' come an' me more than willin' f'double it, when you han' it over to me."

" You sure o' youself, eh ? "

The silence betwixt them got jolt in it. Flea waiting f'Anancy reply. Anancy waiting f'him brain stop spinning circle. This 'frontation got nerves f'both of them, ol' register and new one.

" Whe' you get you money from, Flea ? " Anancy asked tepid.

" Me make me fortune by paintin' people face, like you do, Anancy."

A next jolt catching Anancy. This time so, Anancy near bawl out surprise, but he hold himself back when he thinking about the ol' register and the manners it call for. Instead, he ask Flea to come with him into him big studio. Flea accep'. They walk together in a tight-up silence. The tactics had was to change on Anancy side and he know it like nothing else. The surprise not gentle. Anancy hate getting jump by anything or anybody, least by a' unregister flea. Register mean total everything in Anancy world reckoning, and to stand up and see it getting defile, ignore and surpass making him most insecure bad and almost panic-up, like say it come to bump that class done f'all time. Certain things here f'stay, Anancy well believing so, and he know that that got to be the truth about spider society, don' care what happen. And that belief is the back bone of f'him 'losophy and ambition. The threat fling by Flea is a hard one that no ordinary register spider can stomach. It be a' international revolting thing, a' upheaval business that could cause history to get write over different. Anancy not foolish. He realising mix-up. He seeing collapse going come, and he not liking it. So, when he and Flea get to the big studio entrance, Anancy standing military and allowing Flea to go in first. Flea laugh quiet, and to that flea stroke of newness, Anancy bowing grace and ol' world.

" Who you paint? " Anancy ask, after he pour Flea and himself a society sherry thing.

Flea say : " Anybody."

Anancy : " Like who so ? "

Flea : " Like giants."

Anancy get a third jolt in him ribs, when he hear that piece of news. This Flea causing revolution. Anancy swallow him spit and learning.

" I see," Anancy say.

" Me glad you see, Anancy. Now wha' 'bout me offer, eh? Flea goin' get him face paint by you or not? "

Anancy feeling him territory getting seize. The lan' breaking up and total everybody going own it. The status Q gone like 'vaporation, when sun catch the damp after rain fall and done. So, Anancy say : " Jus' hol' on, Flea. Whe' you make you contacts? " As he say so, he put up him left hand and stop Flea from answering. Anancy feeling confuse. He having a sensation of worry-head and social tormentation to know that a' ordinary flea, from down so, climbing in him own field and making fortune quiet as ever, as the best international, if it come to that. Anancy put some brakes on him wildness and ask question again, but this time, he make it casual and sort of no 'count in

137

the scheme, as if he don' want Flea to answer it at all. Any way, it bring right result. This the way Anancy actual put it: " Who, f'instance, you paint? "

" Well, Anancy, I paint plenty face, like Giant Unicorn, Giant Springbok, Giant Eagle, Giant Bull Dog and Giant Double-head Eagle. Why you askin'? "

Jolt catch Anancy again. But he still nice cucumber on the outside. Hear him : " You paint those face, eh? "

" Yes, man."

" When that? " Anancy more cucumber now.

" Different time, you know. F'instance, I paint Giant Unicorn in Augus'-September."

Anancy say : ' But I paint him in July-June." He stop himself and start over. " I mean I do him in June-July." He losing little cucumber sudden.

" Yes, Anancy. I know that. Let we see : I paint Giant Springbok in March-April-May. He take a whole 'eap o' sittin', you know. Mos' res'less."

" I paint Giant Springbok in December year before, into January-February this," Anancy say. A big slab of cucumber get knock way f'good. He shaking.

" Yes, Anancy. I know that, too. Now, goin' on to the nex' commission them I got : Giant Eagle in September; Giant Bull Dog in December; an' Giant Double-head Eagle also in December. Real good mont', December. Mos' prosperin'."

Anancy knowing now what what. He seeing the broad daylight f'what it doing to him. He planning and double resolve to keep himself calm and capture back him cucumber. Cucumber win battle. Hot head throw way winnings every time. What he got to do now is f'drag out Flea clever as he can do it under the new set of 'stances. Times changing. Anancy know he got to swing with the new. Hear him : " I paint Giant Bull Dog an' Giant Double-head Eagle in the same said November, before you do them in December."

" That I know, Anancy," Flea say.

They looking like firm friend them in club arm chair and saying nothing f'a short embarrass' spell. Yet Flea still calm as first; Anancy not too over-calm at all. Thing to lose, and he losing them.

138

Then Anancy say : " You know somet'ing, Flea, pattern in all this business we talkin' "bout. Don' you t'ink so? "

" Yes, o' course, Anancy, man. I know it got pattern. It got composition, 'tructure an' colour in it too."

Anancy consider him nex' speech. He smile a club smile, full up of live and let live, and cool sweet cucumber. Then he say : " It mean, Flea, that all f'me client them commission me before they commission you. They go to you after they get paint by me. I wonder why? "

" Question, Anancy ! " Flea dead easy.

" Why you come to me knowin' that f'me own top class client them not satisfy with f'me work? "

" Question again, Anancy ! " Flea too cool.

" Wha' you make o' it? "

" You see, Anancy : it obvious, like water, that you not a good painter as me, an' yet still I want you do f'me face picture."

Anancy shaking now. Hear him coming back : " Flea, you only repeatin' wha' I sayin'. Give me idea why you choosin' me." At last, he get cut way from him cucumber. The voice raising Cain. Pride mash up. It gone f'a long no-return walk. Anancy looking like a mixture of curious and hot temper. He swallowing violence and hate and class. He the centre of a high close battle area. He having Flea as a jump-up cuffee showing him new light, and it blinding him. He reeling round and round in him dream-time ol' world, and at the end, he dispossess and empty.

Flea chuckle a wicked chuckle and say : " I mus' beg you not to worry too much, Anancy, if I be you. It quite simple, you know. Painter got to paint, as long as he call himself painter. Painter them come from all 'bout, top, middle, bottom. Bottom mus' come 'pon top, if it a rule that t'ings spin circle. An' another t'ing, Anancy : the business o' bein' a giant is a pure matter o' 'pinion. Giant big an' giant can small, too."

Anancy take the telling and lap him tail, humble and complete rub out. He feeling f'him ol'-time self, but it not there no more. It get lick way foreign. But something still bothering him. He frowning and say : " But why you choose me, Flea? "

Flea do a thing with him shoulders and say : " Don' know meself. Maybe f'see 'ow the other 'alf does do it, an' 'ow it get way wit' it f'so long. Who know? "

And same time as Flea say that, Anancy know that he got invade and conquer, one time, vap!

ANANCY, DON'T GIVE UP!

ANANCY, DON'T GIVE UP!

Anancy one deggeh hope is the single fact that he believe love still existing in the world, at large, all over. He console himself that, at least, love not the one thing that get snatch way from the million Man-Woman family who moving all about the place, ramming and butchering and licking them lip. Anancy been known to walk up to a spider brother and say: "They don' take it way from we yet, eh?" And the brother would nod nervous and broke him neck to move on before Anancy could expan' the question. Anancy always doing that thing to spider people passing him on the road. This way so, he consoling himself that life actual wort' living, even if it a life speckle with red ink. When he not certain how him position stay, as the last remaining believer in love, he go and knock the door of a member of the spider parliament and ask him: "It still at large, don' it?" and the MSP would say cautious: "It all depen' 'pon wha' you mean." And Anancy would expan' and say: "I certain know wha' I mean. You know wha' you mean?" and the MSP reply come: "Well, yes. Tha's if we meanin' the same t'ing." Then Anancy would wise up himself, like lightning and thunder, and fling back to the MSP that, o'course, he mean the same said thing. The MSP would cough a real rockstone parliament cough and pause little bit before he dip into him ol'-time bag-o'-tricks. Pure formula catching Anancy now. After the MSP steady off himself, like a promising cabinet person and smile a pretty constituency laugh, he would say: "Natural, we meanin' the same t'ing. We talkin' 'bout the state o' t'ings to come." But Anancy recognising the spokesman dodge he getting from the MSP and realising it too quick f'the MSP liking. Then, just so, he would say the crippling thing he know going make the MSP helpless complete: "The bigges' t'ing is love."

"Peace bigger," the MSP say.

"'Ow we goin' get peace wit'out tryin' f'love firs'?" Anancy want to know.

"Not'ing try; not'ing get accomplish; tha's wha' I say."

143

But Anancy ready f'him man now. He clear him throat deep barrister and say: "You tellin' me that love reachin' those in need? Like them that out there so, wit'out 'tection? Those that lock up in camp 'pon animal reserve? Those in foreign lan' who not able f'go back to them own 'omelan'? Those who gettin' them righteous revolution tamper wit'? Those who 'ave f'go on wanderin' roun' the worl', searchin' f'a 'ome wit' them own safe back yard, so them don' get molestation from border people an' nex' door neighbour?"

The MSP smile a terror smile and excusing himself as a particular busy man, commit plenty and such like. Then he move off with a vengeance.

Anancy knife sharp brains continuing cut way things to find love underneat'. He got a devotion, something terrible, f'international love, and all day long, he spinning fine thread in him head. Time and so, he feeling that the world can't be nothing but a month-to-month joke thing. He taking up to writing DON'T GIVE UP on scrap paper, and throwing them way or leaving them round the place f'people to pick up and read. One such day, he leave two DON'T GIVE UP sign notes on a Chinaman counter and hide himself safe to see the effect they going have on the first customer who pick them up. He didn' have no long wait. Two confirm smoker them come in, and sure as bauxite get t'ief way, they seeing the notes and reading them curious. One turn and say flat: "Now, who would a want fool we like this?" The other confirm smoker say: "Search every which part o' me!" And they buy them cigarette and walk out with the notes screw up f'the gutter outside. Anancy shake him head at the blindness and walk way like a prophet in him own back yard.

After the Chinaman shop let-down, Anancy go home and sit down in him considering chair and try find himself, real, and lef' hand reflection in the mirror 'cross the room. He thinking about the back-to-front face part of it, too. When he get that far out 'pon the cliff, he calling himself back and starting again with the lef' hand reflection. Night come and catch Anancy dreaming a dream about hope, and he wake up bawling out him guts about how he believe that future living going have hope and love merge up with one force. As if he giving himself lecture in the dark, he not too frighten now. But he sounding, most severe, as he speaking this line, loud, to the lef' hand reflection of himself, to the actual presence of himself and to the presence of the furniture in him spider room : hear him : " Sacrifice the lamb an' save the worl' from itself ! " And then he set him eye, f'a while, on the nice feelings he can get out of imagining. Sleep lick him down, and the room stay like a coffin thing wrap round him breathing body 'pon the spider bed.

When he wake up, in the early part of sun-hot, he searching him head f'a message, f'a sort of Today Message, and only finding yesterday own. He smile a hard smile and squeeze him belt buckle tight, f'the long day lay down before him. He eat breakfast slow, and the next thing he do is making a whole heap of DON'T GIVE UP notes. He make them grand and cautious. He pause between them, lick him spider mouth, write some more, breathe sureness 'pon them and finish cool. Who he going send them to? How much people going think them got meaning f'them? All these champion question bothering Anancy like bitch. He wondering how f'push him notes 'pon the wishy-washy spiders in the Area. He summing up the mentality, foreign plenty and local little bit. He summing up the rich and poor thing. Then he summing up the brightness the lan' always getting shower with from advertisement and newsmongering. Sudden, he realise that the morning burning way like raffia.

He leave the house and head out f'the crowd walking mad round the Area. He patting the bundle of DON'T GIVE UP notes and counting him strides, knowing that he getting near the ending. He make up him mind not to force anybody hand. He going depend on the people them accepting him short notes, just so, without any set hand or ol'-time tactics. So, he decide to play it dead easy. The first 'countering with somebody go something like so. One man saying : " Why you issuin' t'ings like them, anyway? "

' To make people take care o' themself."

" F'wha' so? "

" F'love."

" Then 'ow these notes o' any use? "

" They goin' give those wit'out 'ope new lease 'pon life. They

145

goin' buil' courage, like bridge, an' decen' action, like river, 'mongst we."

The man in the Area street looking at Anancy with sympathy eye and 'nough proper misunderstanding of the message, and say : " You know wha' you can do? You can count me out to rass."

Anancy did want f'ask the man what make so, but he didn' have the heart. The man move off, and Anancy turn opposite to him and walk way hoping 'gainst hope f'buil' up courage and decen' action in plenty people and get them back to them formerly state of beautiful self, so that love could get revive up again. He walk and he get ignore, left and right. He smile, but that don' help him. He look like grave digger to see if that would catch the people them eye and turn it off from the buying and selling thing, but money consideration strong as poison in them belly. As burden holding Anancy down, he take the fact to heart that he can't win, and so he head out f'the public garden and decide himself that he going sit tight and look 'pon himself and catch a glimpse of the world, as it passing inside in him head. As he coming near a' empty bench where he going sit down, he spying three, four tramps talking to one another. He go straight past the bench. He pretending he looking at some red roses. He begin listening to the tramps them. They talking like people who get soak, but who honest to the bone, all the same. One complaining about the bad manners of today children. Another one backing him up saying that today children born without parents. And a next one trying him best to mash that up by saying that parents not necessary at all; he say that other things take over from today parents. He calling the things police force, five-day-a-week school, army, navy, air force and ads. The others chuckling and spitting some phlegm careless as ever. After that, they turning them head to matters that got something to do with the spider State. Anancy listen and hot up himself 'gainst them ideas concern with sadness of all outside people in the world. And then is when he know that he had was to drop him DON'T GIVE UP notes 'pon the tramps them. So, he do so. And then he learning that the tramps don' have no love. They straying and poor, which true as ticks, but they not walking foot and looking love, no how. As a fact, they searching f'things that

146

can swap place with love. Anancy finding out say that they long time give up the wants to buil' up love 'pon a' Islan'-wide scale. They give up them plans to fix up love 'pon a Worl'-wide scale as well.

These things making Anancy feeling salt, like say is nothing but thorn in the public garden where he standing, instead of roses. He see the tramps tearing up the DON'T GIVE UP notes, and he see them scattering the pieces like wedding paper. But wedding don' go so at all. He walk and know that he soon come and find what he looking for. He leave the public garden and bounce him way down the road like a young boy playing board horse. He stop two, three people but nobody want believe in the notes. He start reading the people them face as they coming up close like book. But he reading terror. He reading worries, night and day. And he reading one big fat O. He hold the notes tight.

At last he reach a spot where he sitting down. He ease himself into a day dream and he seeing mad things flitting 'cross him screen. He reaching a hand to touch a nice cup and saucer come from foreign. The sugar sweet. But the saucer melt into a hand and it hold on to f'him own hand. He feeling a free friendship thing with himself. He thinking he know himself. Meantime, the cup melting and shaping itself into a boy child face. The face green and smiling a picture. Then the boy child face grow into a boy countenance. Then into a man own. Then little after, into an ol' man monkey face. The hand pull way itself from Anancy fist and it holding on to the ol' man face. It begin to squeeze it and pat it into one lump of clay. Then the hand get catch with clay, and it coming and forming a lump. Anancy reach out and try a grab f'the two lumps. They shift position and Anancy shift position, too. Sudden lightning and the lumps forming themself again into a cup and then a saucer. And Anancy sighing cool breeze. He rock little bit to the left and then the right and find himself wedge betwixt two structure. He finger them. He rub them. Then he grab them and know what they be. He lift himself ginger and start off on him journey, hoping to hand out him DON'T GIVE UP notes where he find ready hand and eager heart.

And you know what? He find a ready hand. You can't call

147

the heart part anything yet, 'cause it don' show itself, bap, first time. The ready hand belong to a woman Anancy notes capture complete. She nice and young, and her blood and body calling loud and natural like is a beckon finger-post pointing direct in you face. She read the note and talking slow in a whisperish voice to Anancy. Next thing, she and Anancy move off two peas in a pod. Anancy shock that he actual get himself a willing piece of flesh, but he shock absorb the thing nice as ice. She asking him to follow her back to her yard where they able talk private. She explaining that street chat don' buil' anything wort' salt, only confusion and bad spirit. Anancy agree like whip tail. He feeling sharp.

When they get to the yard, the woman tell Anancy what she name. She say she name Mira. Things buil'ing up going on easy. Mira making herself into hostess, and fussing little bit. The high treatment drop Anancy head into doubts, but that not going last long. She give him a bitch drink. He nod back and she sit down beside him. Anancy say thanks and knock it back like foolishness. She jump up and give him another one quick, as if nothing happen. He drink it one time, and she beam a light 'cross her face.

" You's a liquor man," she asking him. " 'Ow you feelin'? "

" Mos' comfo'table, t'ank you, Mira."

Pressure reaching them and silence lumping itself down beside him and her; in fact, horse dead and cow fat talking take holiday. That going on f'a time, and out of nowhere, Mira throat tickling her.

She say : " You do anyt'ing else 'sides givin' way them notes o' yours? "

Anancy calm no cocoa leaf now. He cotton at last to how she stay in her mind. He say : " No. I don' do not'ing else."

" 'Ow you live? "

" I manage."

" You got you own mash-mash? "

" You can call it that, yes."

They moving nearish together and them eyes making four f'the first time. She looking at him and seeing a different sort of man, a man who looking like he going break ground somewhere, like pioneer and so. He looking at her and seeing a good woman

148

with plenty question to ask. He search him head. Then he sure now that she got goodness in her face. Part of the mystery of things shifting, and he taking him ease. He say to himself quiet like that he not seeing the whole of her story, but the part he witness he like. Everybody got some ol'-time history bury up inside; so the world go. But things smooth.

It getting near the time f'Anancy to say goodbye, and he don' know 'nough about Mira at all. He watch her hand and he wondering how he going tackle the thing. Her set-up look nice. She go on like any usual woman with man company. She even get on like she older than him, like how plenty other woman get on with them man and boy. After a while, he know that he in Mother Lan', and he resenting it to rass. He don' like woman suffocation. He always having a mother shadow hanging back o' him head, directing traffic and such like. But he get to know how to dodge it like ace. And it still steal up 'pon him and bite him in him soft parts, just so. He beg him nerves f'stay steady, but they jangling like john crow bead.

Mira ask him : " You want? "

" Wha'? " Anancy say.

" You want lovin'? "

Anancy say : " I believe say that love still exis' in the worl', yes. They don' take it way from me yet. Life wort' livin'."

Mira shake her head and take woman consolation, 'cause she know that Anancy not understanding what she ready to give him.

As that going on in her head, Anancy looking deep. He studying her. He not seeing anything. He looking, but he seeing no shape, no body, just a heap of small chains.

Mira bounce into him and he back into another room and crunch himself down into a chair. She glide up to him and stand stock. He look up and wait. She worm up to him face and shake herself. He search for her body, but he not finding a thing that stay so. He look better, but he not finding no flesh, no body, no Mira. She ups and throw herself 'pon the floor. She say : " Cover me up wit' you notes."

He don' know what to do, even though she talking plain as day. He 'custom to writing the notes. He 'custom to work hard as bitch. He 'custom to plenty worries. Long hours with so-so bad luck. No praise. No outside help. Scraps f'lunch. Sometimes, not a supper is a supper. But this Mira is a different, different thing. He sit down. He scratch him head. He stand up. He sit down again vup. He 'quint. Bird flying coop. He pull the string, and the bundle loose. He pat the bulk and wonder why he doing it.

Mira say : " You ready yet? "

Anancy ignore her. He getting to be suspense father, right 'pon the spot. He liking the role.

" Come, nuh ! " she say.

" Why you want me cover you, Mira? "

Anancy rub him eye. Mira shake herself and step out of her chains and stand up naked in front of Anancy. He turn way him eye. She twist him face round and hold it direct 'pon her skin. He put down the notes beside him and pat them. They bulky and warm bad under him finger.

Mira bathing but Anancy not watching. She order him, like officer, to look 'pon her. He promise. But he not going look. She splash. Anancy not watching. She order him, like officer, again. He promise. She getting wicked. She stand up and Anancy stand up too. This make Mira heart leap. But Anancy saying quite plain that water and borning go together. Both standing toe to toe, like danger, but they not making four with them eye. The bodies making contact and bristling like wire. Mira nakedness dripping. She haul on a' Adam and Eve dressing wrap, apple and fig leaf all over the place; then she leading the way back to the sitting room. She reach her rope end. She take 'nough of Anancy blind eye treatment. She say : " Time you go ! "

He nod, collect him DON'T GIVE UP notes and left Mira standing up in her Adam and Eve dressing wrap. He relieve and thankful no end. But he not showing it, 'cause of bad manners. He walk and walk and thinking about Mira, 'til he run out of wondering how she come so. The bird fly back inside.

Anancy hold him head down and press him foot 'pon the sidewalk to feel him escape. He sudden know that he don' escape at all; all he do is retreat like priest. The bulk of notes coming like consolation. He tighten him grasp. As he turning last right f'the main road, he hear a cry f'help coming out of the last house on the road. He run like a fireman. He hear the cry again. He double up and get to the house in nothing flat. The front door stay open. He go in and the door close behind him bup! A voice say: " Come over yah so." He go to it. Standing up there and waiting f'him is Mira all over again; she got on the Adam and Eve dressing wrap. Anancy blink and swallow hard. He telling himself that love can take this.

Mira glistening like lamp moth under light bulb. She calm and pack up with plans f'Anancy downfall. He feeling like wool covering him. He itch and scratch. He make a move to talk, but she flash out a fork' tongue. She say: " Don' bother tell me. You don' understan'."

" I don' understan'," Anancy say.

" Simple t'ing, man. You see: I always in two place same time. Is so I do it, special when t'ings low wit' love, if you follow me meanin'."

" I not followin'."

" I know so." She start walking in a circle in front of him f'a little while, and then she stop and stare over him head and hold it like camera. She doing all this 'pon tiptoe, as Anancy bending down. He wondering about her, but he not saying a thing. Then she scream out : " Get up."

He get up and move like he walking in him sleep. Mira bark a next order, and he jump. Then she tell him to take off him clothes in the far left hand corner of the room. He do it in a deep dream. She slip out of her Adam and Eve and walk to the dead centre of the room.

" Lick me skin," she say.

Anancy not making a move. Mira bark again. Anancy dead. He stock. Mira not going get beat and she know it. She soften. Drop number eleven.

" Come yah so," she say sweet.

Anancy walk slow to her and 'member to keep him eye 'pon floor level. She tell him to look up. He do it without looking. Mira disappoint no end. She naked and getting ignore which like saying that peel mango in disgrace, 'cause it stay without somebody pick it up and eat it. She tell Anancy to pull the bulk of notes. He ask why. She blaze into him, and he back way from her. She snatch the notes from him and drop them 'pon the dead centre of the room. She peel off the top note, look at it

151

narrow and give Anancy a bad smile. She don' wait f'him answer back. She smile again and put the top note straight back 'pon the bulk. All now, she making Anancy nervous. She walk into him. She bounce him. Then she hug him venomous. He feel a snake. He shiver. She pull way from the snake, back out from him and wait. Nothing. She throw down herself flat in front of him. He stand up over her and tremble like tissue paper under blow nose. He not looking down. She call him name like ceremony. He grunt. She call it again. He grunt again. It coming a ping pong thing.

Mira say : " You know you naked? "

Anancy say : " I know."

" An' you know I naked too? "

" Yes." He start thinking about the subject of loving Mira. She flatten herself 'pon the carpet and play dead.

She raise her head a' inch or so. Her stomach muscle them standing up proud no wash board. Her forehead wet. Her hair paste down. She looking brittle and bringle. " Come, nuh," she say. " I waitin' 'pon you sweetness."

Anancy groan. Nothing else happening in him head. He not feeling a thing.

" Take up you notes them ! "

Anancy move cute. He collect the notes and turn to her. He look down this time. She notice him and smile little bit. He not saying nothing. He feeling dead.

" Drop them 'pon me! "

Anancy shower her front with the notes. He do it with a slow spider sprinkle. She not moving. He look a blessing of looks and say nothing. Her face cover complete with the notes, and she look dead. Anancy not feeling 'sponsible at all. Sudden, Mira shout from underneath the pile of DON'T GIVE UP : " Fall down 'pon top o' me an' take me."

Anancy wishing to him heart that he could do jump-down. He tense up, but it don' come to nothing at all. He bite him mout' corner. Nothing happening.

" Bugguyagga ! " Mira bawl out. " Fuck me, I say. Wha' you waitin' fo'? "

A strong hand hold him shoulder and shake him, and he hear

a voice saying: " Move on. You can't expec' f'do that sort o' t'ing right yah so."

Anancy jump up, bounce himself betwixt the two tall concrete structure and seeing them as lamp post. The policeman smile Babylon and walk off.

The bird shake in Anancy head two time. He smile as he notice that him DON'T GIVE UP notes blowing all over the place. The street and sidewalk litter with them. Everybody picking them up and catching a read same time, north, south, east and west.

Anancy feeling empty. Something that don' have no sense coming into him life. The job done, and he know he don' have anything left f'do. Right then and there, things beginning to look thin. Love funny bad.

ANANCY NOT NO PYAA-PYAA SPIDER MAN
COME FROM BALCARRES F'GET A GARDENER
JOB FROM A BROWN 'OMAN LIVIN' IN A BIG
OL'-TIME BOA'D 'OUSE UP A SAIN' ANDREW
TOP

ANANCY NOT NO PYAA-PYAA SPIDER MAN COME FROM BALCARRES F'GET A GARDENER JOB FROM A BROWN 'OMAN LIVIN' IN A BIG OL'-TIME BOA'D 'OUSE UP A SAIN' ANDREW TOP

Anancy wife say to Anancy, one day, when sun hot in them yard in Balcarres, that is time, now, that Anancy start bettering himself, like how Zacky and Man Boy and Cephas and Macky did go way and fix up themself in 'Merica and Englan', some year aback. But Anancy look straight down 'pon the sun shining out of a condense milk tin and know to himself that he not going pick 'pon either 'Merica or Englan'. When story pop, he got him eye fix 'pon the Sain' Andrew people same place where he living in the Islan'. He like short travel and short catch. As he name Anancy, he got to do things f'him own way. Him wife don' like this sort of contrary business he usual go on with at all.

She say: "Wha' wrong wit' 'Merica an' Englan', Anancy?"

He say: "Them don' 'ave the riht sort o' weat'er an' right mind."

She say: "None o' we go way f'the weat'er an' the mind o' the people who live over foreign. We usual go way f'the money we can work. Not so?"

All he say to that speechifying is: "Money right yah so, special down by Sain' Andrew top."

Anancy wife hold her head and swallow her spit. That is how she living and getting on with her spider man up in the Balcarres bush. Hard head not into it! She got a real difficle man dealing with. All the same, she know how f'pull him in and f'let him out like sea weed playing puss with shipwreck dregs down a' sea bottom. But Anancy not no fool. He catch on to how she handling him from long time, and he knocking sof'ly, so g'long, week in, mont' out, like he can't mash wife. But Anancy not no mampawla; he have balls that hairy same way like any man else own; he just cool with f'him own.

The one thing that worrying Anancy wife is how the Sain'

Andrew people them usual get on, where morals concern. "Them brown people too funny, you 'ear," she saying to Anancy and the other spider man them living round Balcarres. "Them morals gone. Them take 'oliday an' gone f'good."

Anancy not having any bothers about missing morals and all that. He business about money and making it up a' Sain' Andrew. He turn deaf ears every time him wife decide she got sermon f'deliver 'pon the Mount.

So, the day come when Anancy and she s out the spot and leave Balcarres.

When I tell you that Anancy and him wife drop into a new world, I telling you nothing at all that even quarter near the trut'. The set-up in Sain' Andrew different from Balcarres with a vengeance. Balcarres got plenty conceal goodness lock up tight in the ol' ground, hitch up in the people them head and fasten under everything, everywhere. Sain' Andrew have a good looks but that stop there bap. It have some funny things going on, like say things that got to do with cool studies how f'capture a man brains and how f'put down foot heavy 'pon man neck-string and how f'keep him check and control and eating out o' hand and sucking salt t'rou' wooden spoon and wearing sack clot' and ashes and all so. But Anancy catching on to the gardener work and drinking milk and not counting cow one blast. Him wife catch a servant gal job same place and learning the way things go round the place.

Sudden, one day, the brown 'oman body decide to call, and she clap her eye 'pon Anancy body working in the front garden. He naked down to him waist. Sweat cover him spider back and taking time marking the middle o' him khaki short pants. He looking direct down to the dirt and forking the life out o' it.

The brown 'oman 'pon heat. She licking her mout' like she got Anancy back in her face. She tight up her foot and squeeze Anancy in her mind. The sun hot bad, and she idle and got not a Gawd thing f'do, excep' f'think about her front garden and how it want watering.

Anancy take out him hose and start walking slow 'mongst the fork-up ground he just done dig. He flash the hose-top two time and the coil up piece o' length behind him getting on like

158

snake in the grass.

He hear somebody calling him name, distant like. The voice got a sof' message wrap round it. He drop the hose. When he look hard, he see the brown 'oman standing up smiling 'pon him. It don' take him long f'see that the smile not a' employer smile at all. He put one and one together nex' door and make two, and he ready f'the extra work.

After some sweet hot sun rudeness, Anancy finding that he not doing so much gardening, and a whole heap o' weeds growing fast. So, now, the brown 'oman get another gardener to do the work Anancy not doing, 'cause he servicing her too nice in the 'ouse.

By this time, Anancy jook himself straight inside the set-up. He install like fixture. Him wife catch on to what he doing and she gone back to Balcarres with her head full up with bad blood f'the brown 'oman and Anancy.

But things mapping out good f'him. The brown 'oman starting working f'him interes', like she was a' agent somebody down town. She hand over the big ol'-time boa'd 'ouse to him, and the lan' value 'pon top o' it. The nex' move, hell fire, Anancy make, he take over the 'ouse and lan' o' all the brown 'oman friend them in Sain' Andrew. F'all that benefit that happen, he giving all o' them plenty sweetness when them 'usban' back turn.

So, the spider man from Balcarres setting up himself as property developer cocksman and master spider right round the Islan'. Every spider man hating him and the 'oman them praising him f'fixing them up and f'farting 'pon them take-f'granted 'usban'.

But stock bound to take. Anancy telling him Balcarres conscience that he only going on so wild and loving 'cause he fulling up a space that need fulling up, and that all he really doing is supplying grocery like John Chinaman. As the conscience swallow that, Anancy get emancipate quick, and he pull foot and move brisk. One thing causing the nex' thing to born. Anancy get big as bitch. The whole small Islan' belonging to him. He knowing all this and he keeping him two foot plant into the lan' up to him waist. That is one fact about Anancy progress in the Islan'.

The brown 'oman who firs' employ him still with him too.

159

Him real wife sort o' dead in Balcarres, even though she living on the lan' and getting the name o' Anancy firs' legal 'oman.

When five, ten year gone, and two plan gone with it, it looking like Anancy reaching the stage o' the biggest lan'-leader planner in the world o' lan'-leader planners anywhere at all. All sort o' others visiting him to see how he do it and what he do it with. They notice he not living in no big 'ouse 'pon no hill top; he living right slap 'gainst the people them. They get to understand that he got plenty hopes in flowers coming from dirt one day, and fish from the raw sea round him, and 'nough sweat from the people. They see that he don' operate like he got ol' iron and steel and tech. know-wha', though he collar that same thing from foreign when he think it must get collar' f'him purpose 'pon the Islan'. The visitor them like him style. And Anancy like him own style too. He know he right, and it right f'the Islan' set-up.

So, not a pressure name pressure reaching him f'a long time. Most things blooming like Hope Gardens and making out that Anancy not no pyaa-pyaa spider man come from Balcarres f'get a gardener job from a brown 'oman livin' in a big ol'-time boa'd 'ouse up a Sain' Andrew top.

After some small-time parangles and big-time rungus, Anancy take over Islan' after Islan' that stay round where him own Islan' dey. He get the name Islan'-gatherer. Always he taking these piece o' rock in the name o' the people them, and they like it so. The co-op he obtaining would make you cry with 'nough pride and joy and special envy. Pure people-spider, our Anancy! He couldn't put a spangle-foot wrong, if he want; he couldn't drop it 'pon the bad side o' any line, don' matter what.

Nothing stopping him, now. He keep him head down, studying the lan' careful all the time. He work magic with every scrap he take over. All day long, dirt under him fingernail. Even the brown 'oman had was to tell him that the ground going swallow him one day, if he don' give it a res'. But Anancy laugh and close him eye narrow.

The dreaming start. Nothing but lan' and food covering it. Some chemical and machine get into the set-up too, and wonders working. The lan' turn king. Anancy turn Boss Man o' the king. Things revving.

One night, Anancy get a message to take over all the Islan' them that lef', and all the Continent them in the world. The asking come from the people themself. Anancy lick him mout' and say yes. And so, the world start looking like a garden. Anancy walk over it and clap him hand and say: " Moses, I reach! "

He spend plenty days on one garden call Lidice, and when he leave it, it blooming roses all over. Ace gardener as he know he be, Anancy look round him, when he finish, and eyewater drop out o' him eye and water the roses. That was one set o' gardening that touch him heart deep. Then he spend some more days on another garden call Sahara, and when he leave the ocean o' sand, every drop green no emerald and pushing grass all which way.

Time going on and Anancy working like he got earth fever chronic bad. The strain kill off the brown 'oman complete. So, Anancy send f'him real legal Missis up a' Balcarres. She come 'pon spot and settle down with him nice as peas.

Things moving. Colour green catching fire everywhere. Belly full and mind satisfy. Heart not leaping and heaven come down to ground. But some idle pictures flashing 'cross Anancy eye. He don' have any more place to turn green, or any more dirt to cultivate under him hand. Right away, he feeling like he not ticking like clock proper at all. So, he decide that he got to 'vestigate up yonder, since down here fix up already. He buil' a space craf' and him and him wife take off and orbit catch them. The two o' them going round and round like lignum vitae gig, 'til bamdambam them shoot off into the empty thing over so. And Anancy start getting busy and planning all sort o' new business upstairs. But he not landing anywhere.

He turn to him wife and say: " Look like we run out o' lan', ol' lady."

She smile and say back: " Lan' got to stop some place, Anancy."

But that lick him hard. Lan' is Anancy and Anancy is lan'. So, now, on the journey, he showing that he crumbling way slow in him blood. The wife seeing the change.

161

She say sof' like : " You flakin' way like 'ill side, drought time."

He nod yes.

When the craf' not reaching anywhere solid foreign f'plenty years, and hope not green again, the wife come to her senses and drop some deep argument 'pon Anancy. Hear her : " You find a cute way f'run way from the workin' worl', Anancy."

Anancy vex like rass. He say : " I not runnin' at all. I jus' travellin' an' seein' wha' I seein' lay down roun' we."

" You not 'pon the groun' facin' fac's, man."

" Fac's up 'ere f'face too, you know, 'oman."

" Anancy, you foolin' youself. Up 'ere don' got no fac's as we know them down bottom. Things dark, an' light gone."

Anancy vex worser now. " Who tell you that I not a light-giver, 'oman? "

The wife, even though she legal, shut her mout' one time. She take Anancy measure from the ol' days and she know when to ease up and make him run way cool breeze.

Anancy feeling great. He look outside the craf' and say to himself that the nex' job he got to do is make space light up bright.

Anancy passing a nearish star that burning lick and promise. He know right away that he can use it. He study how he going harness it like horse, even though it not burning bright at all. He collar it, same like how he collar the lan' down a' bottom, and he farm it and work it, 'til it catch fire and blaze like mad-ness. Then he use it and touch up the part o' space he travelling in. And slow but sure, brightness start happening all over the place up yonder. Little more time and Anancy wife feeling proud.

She say : " But, man, you take you fas' self an' changin' up the star them back yard. Is 'ow you come so? "

Anancy laugh two time and say : " I can't 'elp it, you know. Is so I born, an' is so I stay. Not a t'ing name ' can't do ' f'me. Not a t'ing name ' can't change ' either. T'ings make to change an' make to get better."

" You *bad,* sah," the wife tell him straight, her head swelling up as bitch that he so good in him brains.

162

But like how everything in space light up now, Anancy finding out that he don' have anything else to plan to do. He feeling salt. Hear him to him wife: " I reach back where I was, ol' lady. Life too cute."

She say : " I know it would 'appen, yes."

Anancy : " So wha' we goin' do, now? "

" Go back down an' see wha' we see, nuh."

Anancy shake him head and consider the move two, three time. Then he turn round the space craf' and burn up the track back to dutty.

When he nearing the spot, he look through the window and he say : " We should 'ave more than one worl', you know. One worl' too small f'people to live in."

The wife close her eye them and say : " Lock up youself in you 'ead then, nuh, Anancy."

" You t'ink that that could come like another worl'? "

" Is another worl', yes."

So, Anancy decide to do that.

Anancy new world inside him own head sort o' difficle. It got problem. He not living in there too natural. He fix two world already. But the third one looking like he can't do nothing with it. He make the first one green and thing. He fling light right round space. But the head world beating him.

As all that change going on, the wife taking her time and getting charge o' every Gawd time and space thing that Anancy develop; she take over the Islan' them and the Continents and the space light. Anancy don' have no time to check up 'pon her movements, as he lock up in him head all day long.

Sudden, he start going on funny. The wife tell him, one night : " I been t'inkin' that you better put youself in a special set-up where you can plan a grab 'pon you 'ead. Why you don' lock way youself private an' study you brains? "

Anancy take the advice and lock way himself. The wife throw way the key and burs' a laugh loud, loud. She work hard and release the Islan' them and all the Continents, and she manage send a message up yonder to space telling it to turn off the bright light as it want. Then she get a big everlasting truck and put Anancy and the lock-up thing he living in inside it, and make a bee-line back to Balcarres. When she reach, she let go Anancy out o' the lock-up something, and cotch him up in a big ol'-time cotton tree just outside her front yard.

And, you know something? 'Til this day name day, when you passing there, you can feel the web Anancy spinning touch you face, as he studying how to conquer him brains and make himself powerful can't done.

And, you know something else? When you passing the spot where the web making friend with you face, if you listen good, you can hear a voice laughing a last laugh in the distance. And o' course, I don' have to tell you is who voice you hearing, 'cause it could only belong to one person and one person only, Anancy wife; and the voice legal, too.

A REAL, REAL SHORT STORY AS TO HOW ANANCY ACTUAL REACH UP THROUGH F'HIM ONE WIFE TO EQUAL LIFE WITH ALL TOTAL 'OMANKIND, *BAPS!*

A REAL, REAL SHORT STORY AS TO HOW ANANCY ACTUAL REACH UP THROUGH F'HIM ONE WIFE TO EQUAL LIFE WITH ALL TOTAL 'OMANKIND, *BAPS!*

This Anancy learning that one love is a high signpost on the lan'. He learning that the lan' bigger than himself, same one. He learning that running down him wife and going in for backing-way tactics and kissing way miseries can't solve a rass thing. He learning that live wit' and dey wid mus' be a tree with fruit, or else.

So, he come to himself with this new sharing idea, and he promise that nothing but a different view of wife going fix up the new view of 'omankind deep down inside him head, one time, like say equal life is one love. But the actual learning hard as arse. The ol'-time *macho* sign-posts them still bright bad, all over the hill an' gully 'cross the lan'.

In fac', revolutin' badder hard!

Yet, he knowing that it got to mus' or else the lan' going stay there and dead under him foot, jus' so.

So, now, he take time and trying to reach base and change f'him own ace spider-manhood into pure working spiderness without all the man thing showing like prickle. When he look 'pon 'oman, he seeing her as a pardner, like a throw-han' pardner, equal in the gamble pot 'pon fire. He seeing her so like he seeing f'him own self. That nearly kill him!

It so new! The newness of the thing would all want to choke him it so new and out o' ordinary.

He say to himself, one day, as he sitting watching the harbour water, down by King Street bottom : *But, wait, little bit, now! She favour me, yes. What a way she favour me, in trut'. Me is she. She is me. We is one. 'Ow come the knife separation 'appen? 'Ow it come that the botheration so total an' so deep an' so bitch time past tense amen tie wit' string an' drop into cupboard-draw' an' store 'way? 'Oman same as me an' me into she; me come out o' she, slip back into she, as accordin' to night*

167

an' day, as accordin' to parangles in Q, an' even then, the one-
ness is always more than minutes. What a rass!

Thoughts burs' him head plenty times, as he thinking out the
'oman thing and thinking out the new sharing view, and same
time so, he start to circle out the pattern of the equal condition
which arriving slow and tough bad. It was a process strain that
he never have any training for or any experience of, like how
say f'him spider-manhood didn't reckon on that as a way of
looking at 'omankind and the lan'.

So, after the heaps and heaps o' thoughts, he absolute, now.
He leave the harbour water and face the lan'. He go up by
him wife, and he saying, " I was wrong, you know."

" But, you was always that, Anancy," she tell him, bold face.

" No," he prax back, " that is ol'-yesterday story. Wha' I
mean to say is that I born wrong."

" *You* born wrong, Anancy? " she ask.

" Yes, I born wrong."

She frown up her forehead and say, " Is you say so, 'member,
eh? "

" Yes, I born too wrong," he confirm, like it was a big Coun-
cil talk.

" So, tell me, nuh," she clips.

" Wha' I sayin' is this, now : we's one! " The statement leave
him mout' dry as a chip cup.

Anancy wife smile.

" We's one," he telling her, again.

" But, stop, Anancy? " she haul off and look direct into him
spider face. " I did know that from mornin', you know. I did
know that from when I small. Is only now you find out? "

Anancy quiet like hearse inside. This thing too big for him,
and he tight with it. Is the training he lack. Is the experience
he want. Revolutin' fuck-up bad!

She saying to him, now, " 'Ow you find out? "

He say back to her, " I was by the harbour, you see."

" Plenty things born into water, yes," she chance take.

" No," he say, " I was lookin' at the water spread out far outside the lan', an' I come to measure the one love sayin' in me
own mind. An' it catch me. We's really one into one."

Anancy wife smile, again. " So, 'ow things go, now, from

168

that? " she ask.

" I don' too know rightly but them changin' angle. I seein' more."

" Like wha' so? "

" Like you an' me."

" I goin' 'ave to change, too, then? " she salt back.

" Why? " he want to know.

" Well, because, Anancy, I always see you, you same said one, Anancy, an' every man Jack, as boy, you know."

Anancy like he get sting by bees. He shake. He shudder. He rock back. He swallow hard. " 'Ow so? " He swallow two time again. " I not no boy. Me's a big spider-man, 'oman. You can't see that I's a big man, nuh? "

" Well, hear me," she say, " all o' you is boy to mos' 'oman, you understan'. 'Oman been without equal for centuries. She been 'mongst so-so pickney all her life on the lan'. Some o' you is five year ol' an' some o' you is fifty. Five or fifty, all o' you is boy. So, now that you equal up youself wit' me in you mind, I goin' 'ave to study me head an' change to accep' that rapid growt', yes."

Anancy into puzzlement mother and father! He almost feeling sorry that he did talk him talk.

Yet and all though, the equal thing and one love nice him bad; it sweet him for true. And it showing a tree with fruit that can't done.

169

NEW MAN ANANCY

NEW MAN ANANCY

Most things was looking real ol' and run-down bad, everywhere in the C. World. The lan' was tired. The sea was a dirty thing. The trees have blight. The rivers them stop up. The people was empty and sucked out like three million seeds. Things couldn't be worser.

I mean, down to the sand on the beach, down to it, now, nothing but darkness reaching it, even though the sun up and light catching the Area, like say it was furnace fire. In fac', the condition was close to shut-down and the end.

So much life-living and death-nearness was blocking up Anancy as he looking back over the years in the ol' country and in f'him own new one that he decide to sink the pictures in him head, and look out to the open window, out into the yard, where the generations was jus' catching the sun in the early part o' the day.

Is a new, brandless new man we need, yes! he telling himself. But he got to be brandless. He can't be brand new or else the brand might hol' all o' we to ransom note, one way or the other. Every brand demand payment. Every brand cause a new sort o' enslavement. Every brand want to take you over anxious, turn you into a nex' carbon copy, then spit you out like rotten teet'. Every brand is a brand-mark. So, the brandless new man got to be a man without any chains bangin' round people foot. He got to be a real invention!

Anancy walk gentle and knock 'pon Brother Tiger door. He knock two, three time. Tiger come out looking tired and wise. Anancy say, " Tiger, is 'ow this new man goin' go, eh? I jus' was thinkin' 'bout him in the sun-hot in the yard. Is 'ow him goin' stay 'mongst we? "

Tiger touch him face, like say it was missing, and he say, " Firs' thing, Anancy, is that this new man got to be a real new sort o' hopin' man wit' different appetite, different sort o' hunger, different sort o' in-take o' food, too, an' total different attitude to workin' on the lan' an' dreamin' C. World dreams.

173

That is a mos' vital difference thing, you see. He got to be a new sort o' workin' man on the lan', especial 'mongst the green things them. He got to be, more than anything else, a man who don' 'ave appetite for wha' we 'ave, now, right here so. That's it. The new man mus' want nothing we want as we is now."

Anancy nod and take foot and go by Sister Mysore Cow, and he say to her, " Sister Cow, is 'ow this new man in the sun-hot out in the yard goin' go? "

Sister Cow say, " For one thing, Anancy, he got to born to some early o'clock different trainin' in the yard, in all the yards o' the C. World, so he can grow up different from we, even though is out o' we he goin' born! The thing is this, Anancy : can we do the necessary trainin'? After all, I know say that the new man goin' 'ave to born out o' we same one."

Anancy, he blink hard, jus' nod and say, " But Sister Cow, man, 'ow that goin' go? "

" Life go so, newness or no newness," she say. " Is a thing call process catch we when we wasn't lookin', Anancy. Is a funny thing, process! Everything tie up wit' every nex' thing on the lan'. One new thing born out o' the ol' thing same way. That is the real trouble. The new thing could 'ave a trace an' touch o' ol'ness inside it, jus' waitin' to jump out an' fuck things, voop! But, as life go, trainin' could fix it, yes."

Anancy don' too like how Sister Cow talk. He figure she not out to believe in the new man change, at all, as him believe in it, deep down. He didn' like all her talk about ol'ness tie up with newness, and so. Pure so-so bafflement holding on to him throat, now. So, then, he take a canoe and travel soulful over to Brother Warrior hut.

" Brother Warrior, is 'ow he goin' go? " Anancy ask, shaping the new man with all him spangles. " You is a man who fight plenty war in foreign. You mus' 'ave some particular thoughts to share wit' me."

" Well, Anancy, you's the man who should know, as seein' that you did stay at home when I was over yonder, as seein' that you know the lan', an' as seein' that you do a lot o' life-livin' an' deat'-nearness, all you days. An' listen : I thank you for you buil'-up but is foreign my generation fight for, you know, not for the C. World. Thanks all the same for the buil'-up. Anyway,

174

I would say that this new man you got on you brains, right now, could actual get form in a fire, you know, in a bitch-time fight wit' plenty fire-power wrap round him soul an' body. I mean, fightin' is a good thing to make you or crack you up in splinters. Like 'ow all our people on the lan' jus' sort o' peaceful an' go wit' the book an' like Constitution an' so, for years an' years, an' don' know wha' fightin' is like, I think that a little fire in the new man tail could be a sweet formation thing, yes, for him an' for all o' we."

Anancy back out in the canoe, and row himself to the other side. He jus' couldn't bring him mind to open up to any more suggestions concerning the new man in the C. World, and how he going get form, and what him going look like when he form good and proper.

Weeks. And still the new man bothers continuing for Anancy. A voice suddenly begging him to consider the meaning of the C. World. The voice is a small thing that even Anancy can't stifle, a sort of nagging face up to the shadows voice that simple out of this world and handcuff to Anancy inside mind. Is the sort of voice that ups and say things like, for instance: *A. World make out o' the riches o' C. World; B. World make out o' A. World an' C. World an' C. World make out o' wha' lef, approx. dregs an' leavin's.*

In point o' fac', the C. World is a thing that poor Anancy was always taking for granted, like sun-hot and dusk; but the voice making him feel that examination-time ripe.

So, Anancy make a start, and open out him head to the insides of the C. World, which, after all, is nothing else but Anancy own world.

He get to find out, that is saying, discover with him new eyes, that the C. World is a green world; it have plenty green things, beautiful growing things, things that go in circles, real sweet crop circles, things that inside Nature belly, cool and easy, in spite of the sun-hot. He buck up on the fac' that the C. World is a strong people-world, too, where all the power is people, no matter how them poor, maltreat and develop under, people with a heap o' invention coil up inside them like watch-spring.

175

Slow but sure, Anancy get right slap up against the extra truth that say, as well, that the C. World, like the people into it, need liberate bad. He get to know, as through the new eyes, that that is the release that the coil up watch-spring inside the new man mus' be depending on to break out of the C. World paralysis thing.

He pick up, one time, a coffee tree leaf, and it talk up to him and say, " I grow in this groun' but I belongs, over so, after crop time, an' is all like you, Anancy, that cause that to 'appen to the green things on the lan'."

Anancy couldn't answer the coffee leaf, at all. He try but the try jus' come to ashes.

Then, there was other meetings jus' like that one, and Anancy tongue tie up in all of them. He couldn't say a word to the cane stalk or the banana leaf or the pimento seed or the how much different C. World natural goodness that into the groun' on the lan'. When you hear say that Anancy tongue backward it really backward into silence, as these meetings going on. Then, it get worser, yes !

He leave the surface groun' and start digging into it, and one piece o' red dirt fly up into him face, and let go one accusation 'cross it; it go so, " I make plenty riches under you foot an' you cause all o' it to leave the lan' an' go by foreign. Wha' the rass hole you think this is, at all, though, eh? Freeness or wha'? Is jackass you like play, nuh? Oonuu better lay claim to the dirt an' own it, out an' out, or else is the sea you goin' find youself into, down a' bottom, too ! "

That red dirt talking really educate Anancy in seconds. It mash him up, yes, but it C. back in Q an' remake him an' him mind, same time. He decide, there an' then, to put a little red dirt sample in him pocket and walk round with it for guidance in him search for the new man thing.

The red dirt laugh quiet like when it see Anancy do that, because it recognise that Anancy making a start to lay claim, small as the dirt is that he take up and put inside him pocket.

Anancy, now, decide to take a little retreat from the search, and study him head good. He living in a hut by a river, and he spending plenty hours learning some of the mysteries of the C. World, especial the people, f'him people, including himself; and

176

that go on longer than hours, in fac', to tell the truth. Weeks. Sudden, it was months.

Then, he ready to leave the hut and go back to him people to learn more than the retreat could give him. He come to know that that is where the change bound to mus'; and he fix up him head to study more than ever.

All the time so, the C. World draining way in riches and future. A few of the same people who get high place is the cause, as Anancy analysis get to find out, and he write them down in him mind as HOUSE AND LAN' ENEMY NO. 1.

As soon as he spot them, the other enemy reveal itself like a lantern slide, bright as peeny-wally come evenin' time.

The other enemy was sort of conceal up, firs', but it get clear to Anancy, and he call it OVER YONDER ENEMY WITHOUT NUMBER.

When Anancy meet up with Brother Tiger, Sister Mysore Cow and Brother Warrior, he was feeling more better than ever. He actual feeling that the answer coming soon o'clock. The sister and the two brothers them noticing the change from search to confidence, from questions to answer, from talk to action-start, from C. World ignorance to direct C. World experience and power.

All that please them, no end, especial Brother Warrior.

And needless to tell you : the very first thing that Anancy do was to go straight to him people with a power meeting, the red dirt safe inside him shirt pocket, lay down 'pon top o' him heart.

Brother Tiger say, looking at him 'mongst the people, " You think he find wha' him was lookin' for, Sister Cow? "

Hear Sister Cow, sof', sof', " Yes, I think so, yes. The eyes them showin' it. Wha' you think, Warrior? "

And Brother Warrior say, ' You can't tell jus' so right here an' now all of a sudden, but one thing sure I know is that the new man Anancy is a mos' possible man on the lan' in the C. World, but definite that ! "

Right as that was going on and not too far from where Anancy and the people was holding them first big RED DIRT MEET-

ING, a little boy, who could be Anancy self son, was sitting down by the harbour water and pointing out to a blind beggar-man three o' the biggest A. World ships ever to come into the harbour mout'.

The little boy couldn't hear himself for the power that was coming from the RED DIRT MEETING. The beggar-man, ol' and twist up with mash up development, was jus' nodding him head, as he trying to catch both what the boy telling him about the ships and what the meeting saying to the people.

Final, the ol' man say to the boy, " Sonny, don' bother wit' the ships them. I expec' them to come. Them never too far, never was, from time. You jus' tell me wha' the people an' Brother Anancy sayin' up the road. That's wha' I want to hear."

The boy turn him back on the ships, and fix him ears like telescope on the meeting.